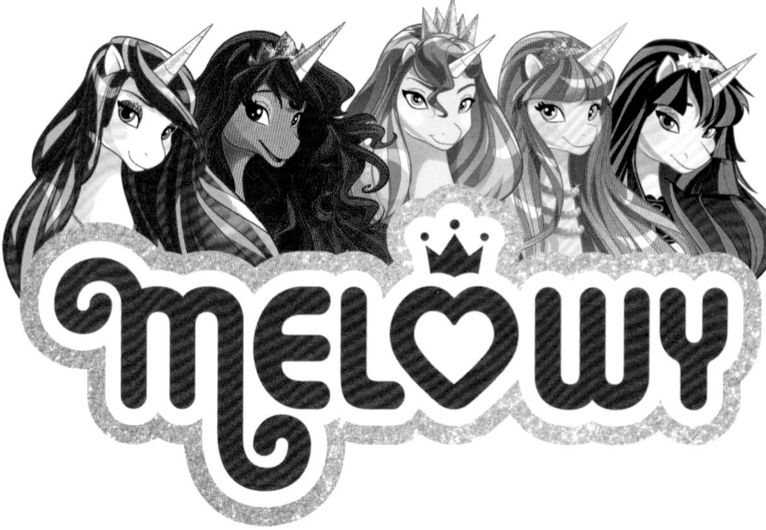
MELOWY

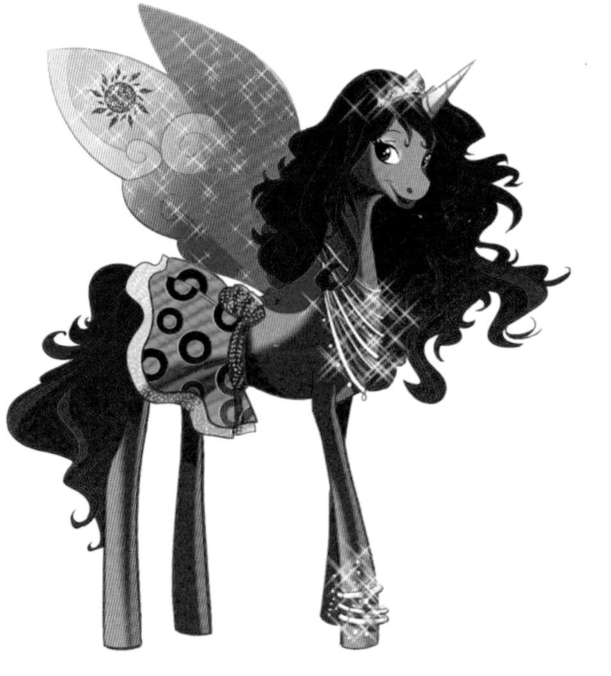

PAPERCUTZ

MORE GREAT GRAPHIC NOVEL SERIES AVAILABLE FROM PAPERCUTZ

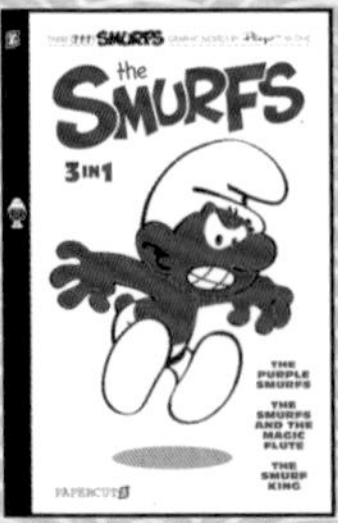

the SMURFS
3 IN 1

THE SMURFS 3 IN 1 #1

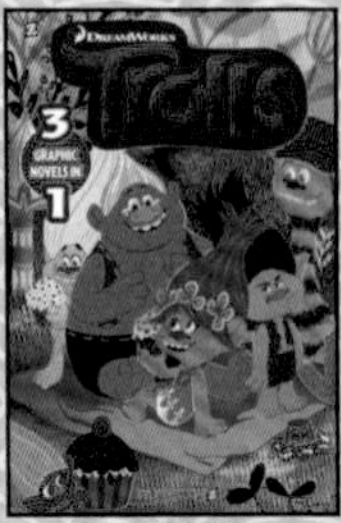

TROLLS
3 GRAPHIC NOVELS IN 1

TROLLS 3 IN 1

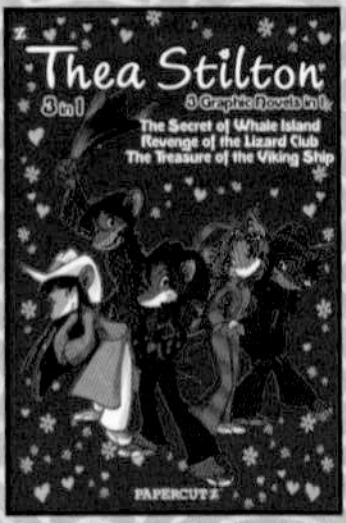

Thea Stilton
3 Graphic Novels in 1:
The Secret of Whale Island
Revenge of the Lizard Club
The Treasure of the Viking Ship
PAPERCUTZ

THEA STILTON 3 IN 1 #1

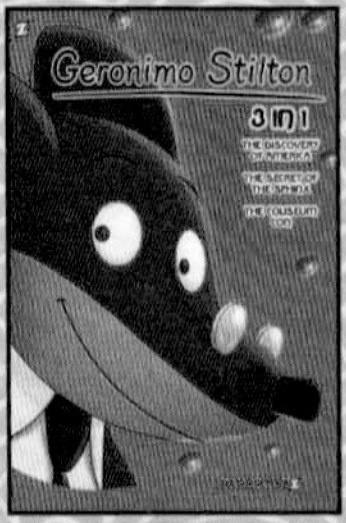

Geronimo Stilton
3 IN 1

GERONIMO STILTON 3 IN 1 #1

COMING SOON

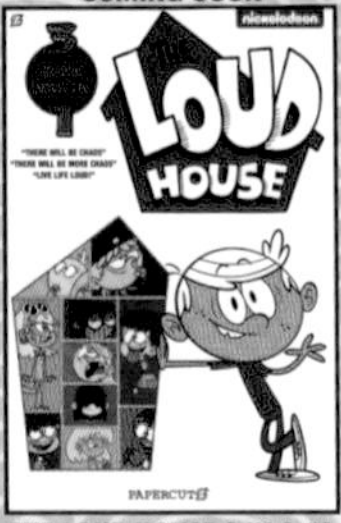

nickelodeon
LOUD HOUSE
PAPERCUTZ

THE LOUD HOUSE 3 IN 1 #1

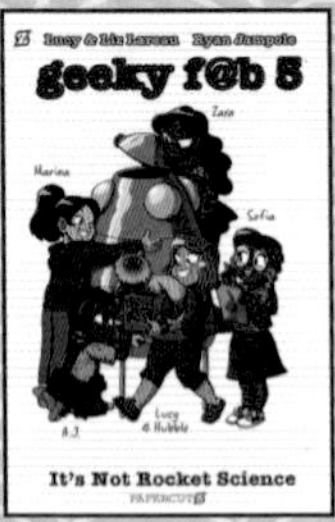

geeky f@b 5
It's Not Rocket Science
PAPERCUTZ

GEEKY F@B 5 #1

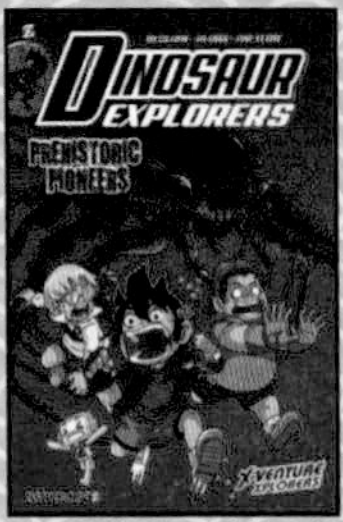

DINOSAUR EXPLORERS
PREHISTORIC PIONEERS

DINOSAUR EXPLORERS #1

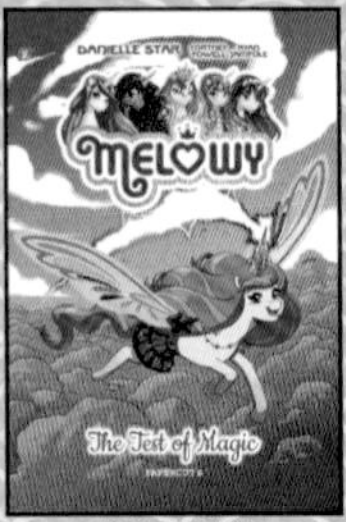

MELOWY
The Test of Magic

MELOWY #1

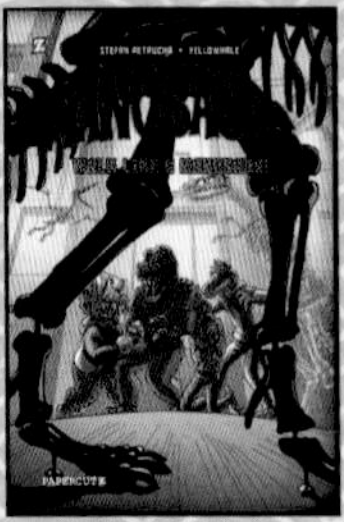

PAPERCUTZ

MANOSAURS #1

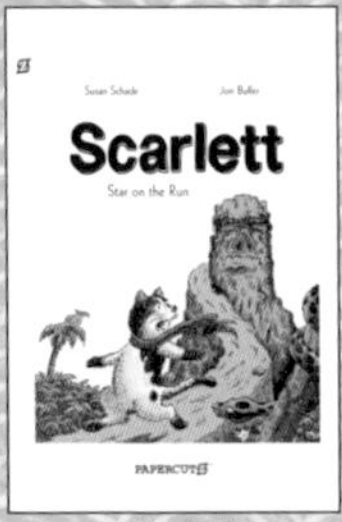

Susan Schade
Jon Buller
Scarlett
Star on the Run
PAPERCUTZ

SCARLETT

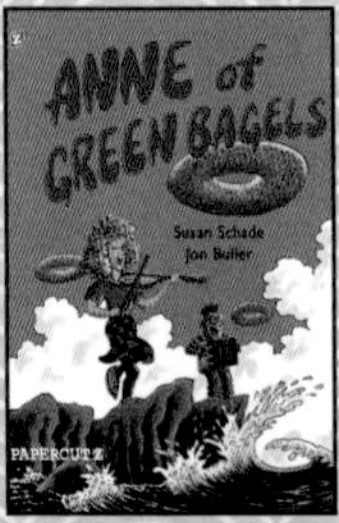

ANNE of GREEN BAGELS
Susan Schade
Jon Buller
PAPERCUTZ

ANNE OF GREEN BAGELS #1

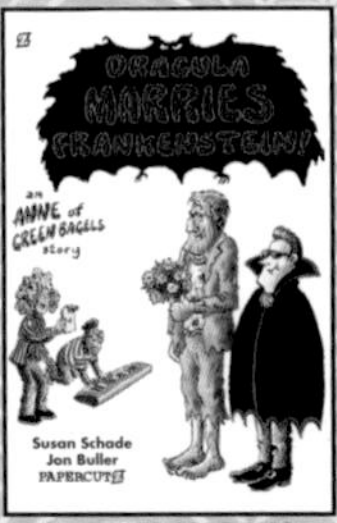

DRACULA MARRIES FRANKENSTEIN!
an ANNE of GREEN BAGELS story
Susan Schade
Jon Buller
PAPERCUTZ

DRACULA MARRIES FRANKENSTEIN!

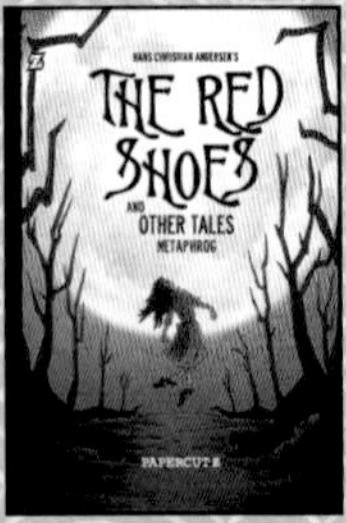

HANS CHRISTIAN ANDERSEN'S
THE RED SHOES
AND OTHER TALES
METAPHROG
PAPERCUTZ

THE RED SHOES

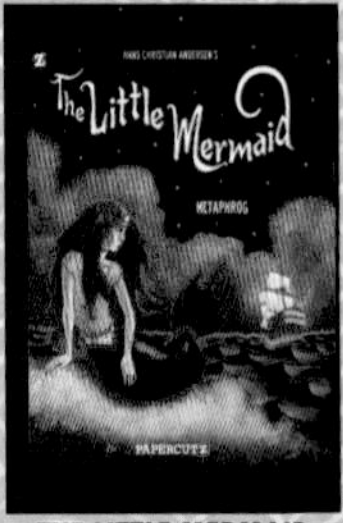

HANS CHRISTIAN ANDERSEN'S
The Little Mermaid
METAPHROG
PAPERCUTZ

THE LITTLE MERMAID

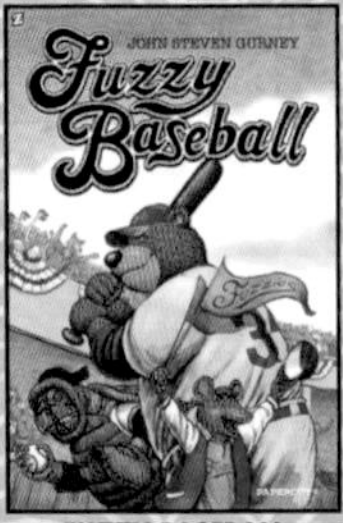

JOHN STEVEN GURNEY
Fuzzy Baseball

FUZZY BASEBALL

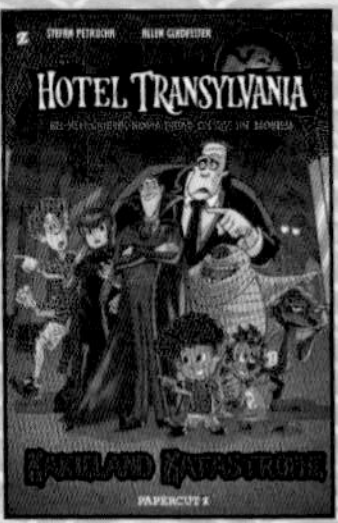

HOTEL TRANSYLVANIA
PAPERCUTZ

HOTEL TRANSYLVANIA #1

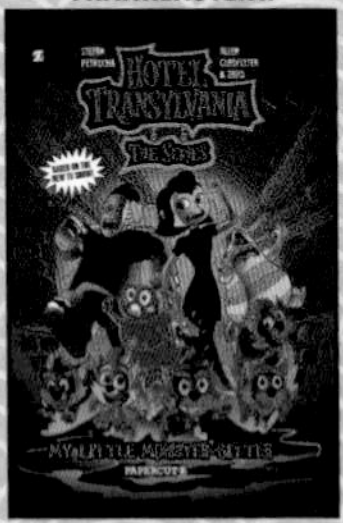

HOTEL TRANSYLVANIA
PAPERCUTZ

HOTEL TRANSYLVANIA #2

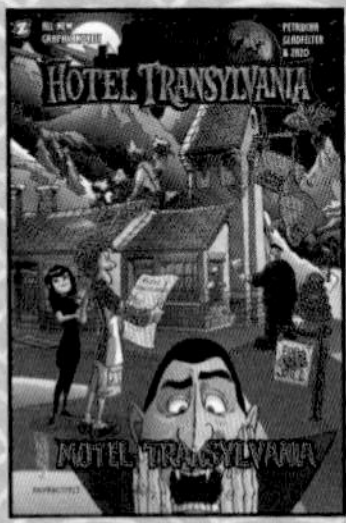

HOTEL TRANSYLVANIA

HOTEL TRANSYLVANIA #3

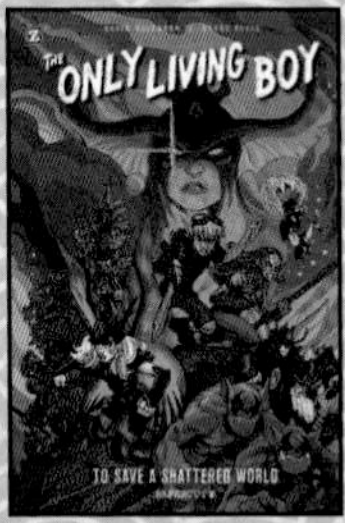

THE ONLY LIVING BOY
TO SAVE A SHATTERED WORLD

THE ONLY LIVING BOY #5

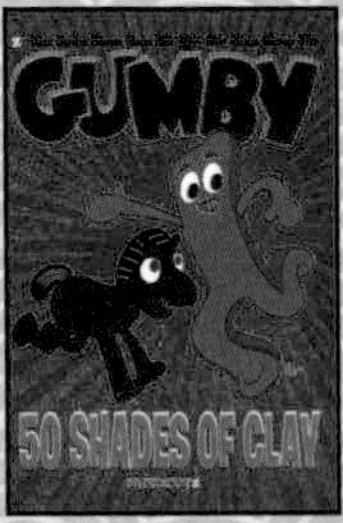

GUMBY
50 SHADES OF CLAY

GUMBY #1

THE SMURFS 3 IN 1, TROLLS 3 IN 1, BARBIE 3 IN 1, GERONIMO STILTON 3 IN 1, THE LOUD HOUSE 3 IN 1, SCARLETT and ANNE OF GREEN BAGEL graphic novels are available for $14.99 each in paperback only. THE ONLY LIVING BOY and GUMBY graphic novels are available for $8.99 each in paperbac and $13.99 each in hardcover. DINOSAUR EXPLORERS graphic novels are available for $12.99 each in paperback and $16.99 each in hardcover. FUZZ BASEBALL graphic novels are available for $9.99 each in paperback only. DRACULA MARRIES FRANKENSTEIN! graphic novels are available for $12.99 each i paperback only. HOTEL TRANSYLVANIA #1 and MANOSAURS graphic novels are available for $7.99 each in paperback and $12.99 each in hardcover. HOTE TRANSYLVANIA #2, HOTEL TRANSYLVANIA #3, GEEKY FAB 5, MELOWY, THE RED SHOES and THE LITTLE MERMAID graphic novels are available for $12.9 each in hardcover only.

Available from booksellers everywhere. You can also order online from www.papercutz.com. Or call 1-800-886-1223, Monday through Friday, 9-5 EST. MC, Vis and AmEx accepted. To order by mail, please add $5.00 for postage and handling for first book ordered, $1.00 for each additional book and make check payable NBM Publishing. Send to Papercutz, 160 Broadway, Suite 700, East Wing, New York, NY 10038.

MELOWY, THE SMURFS, TROLLS, BARBIE, GERONIMO STILTON, THE LOUD HOUSE, GEEKY FAB 5, DINOSAUR EXPLORERS, MANOSAURS, SCARLETT, ANNE OF GREEN BAGELS, DRACULA MARRIES FRANKENSTEIN!, THE RED SHOES, THE LITTLE MERMAID, FUZZY BASEBALL, HOTEL TRANSYLVANIA, THE ONLY LIVING BOY, and GUMBY graphic novels are also available wherever e-books are sold.

The Fashion Club of Colors

Cortney Powell — Writer
Ryan Jampole — Artist
MELOWY created by **Danielle Star**

PAPERCUTZ
New York

MELOWY #2
"The Fashion Club of Colors"

Melowy created by DANIELLE STAR
Cover by RYAN JAMPOLE
Editorial supervision by ALESSANDRA BERELLO and LISA CAPIOTTO
(Atlantyca S.p.A.)
Script by CORTNEY POWELL
Art by RYAN JAMPOLE
Color by LAURIE E. SMITH
Lettering by WILSON RAMOS JR.

Production – JAYJAY JACKSON
Assistant Managing Editor – JEFF WHITMAN
JIM SALICRUP
Editor-in-Chief

ISBN 978-1-5458-0363-9

Printed in China
March 2020

Papercutz books may be purchased for business or promotional use.
For information on bulk purchases, please contact Macmillan
Corporate and Premium Sales Department at (800) 221-7945 x5442.

Distributed by Macmillan
First Printing

THE FASHION CLUB OF COLORS

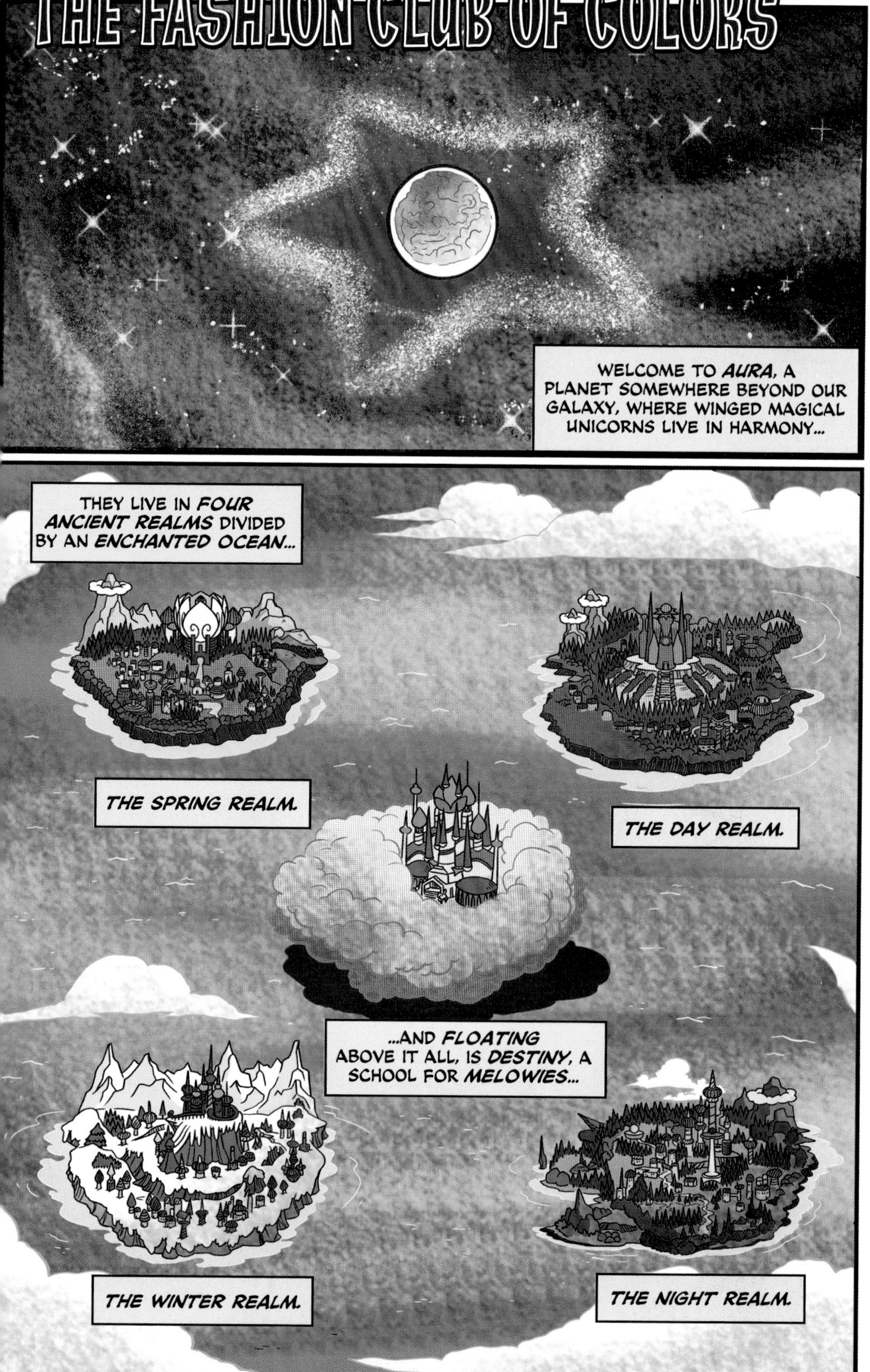
WELCOME TO *AURA*, A PLANET SOMEWHERE BEYOND OUR GALAXY, WHERE WINGED MAGICAL UNICORNS LIVE IN HARMONY...
THEY LIVE IN *FOUR ANCIENT REALMS* DIVIDED BY AN *ENCHANTED OCEAN*...
THE SPRING REALM.
THE DAY REALM.
...AND *FLOATING* ABOVE IT ALL, IS *DESTINY*, A SCHOOL FOR *MELOWIES*...
THE WINTER REALM.
THE NIGHT REALM.

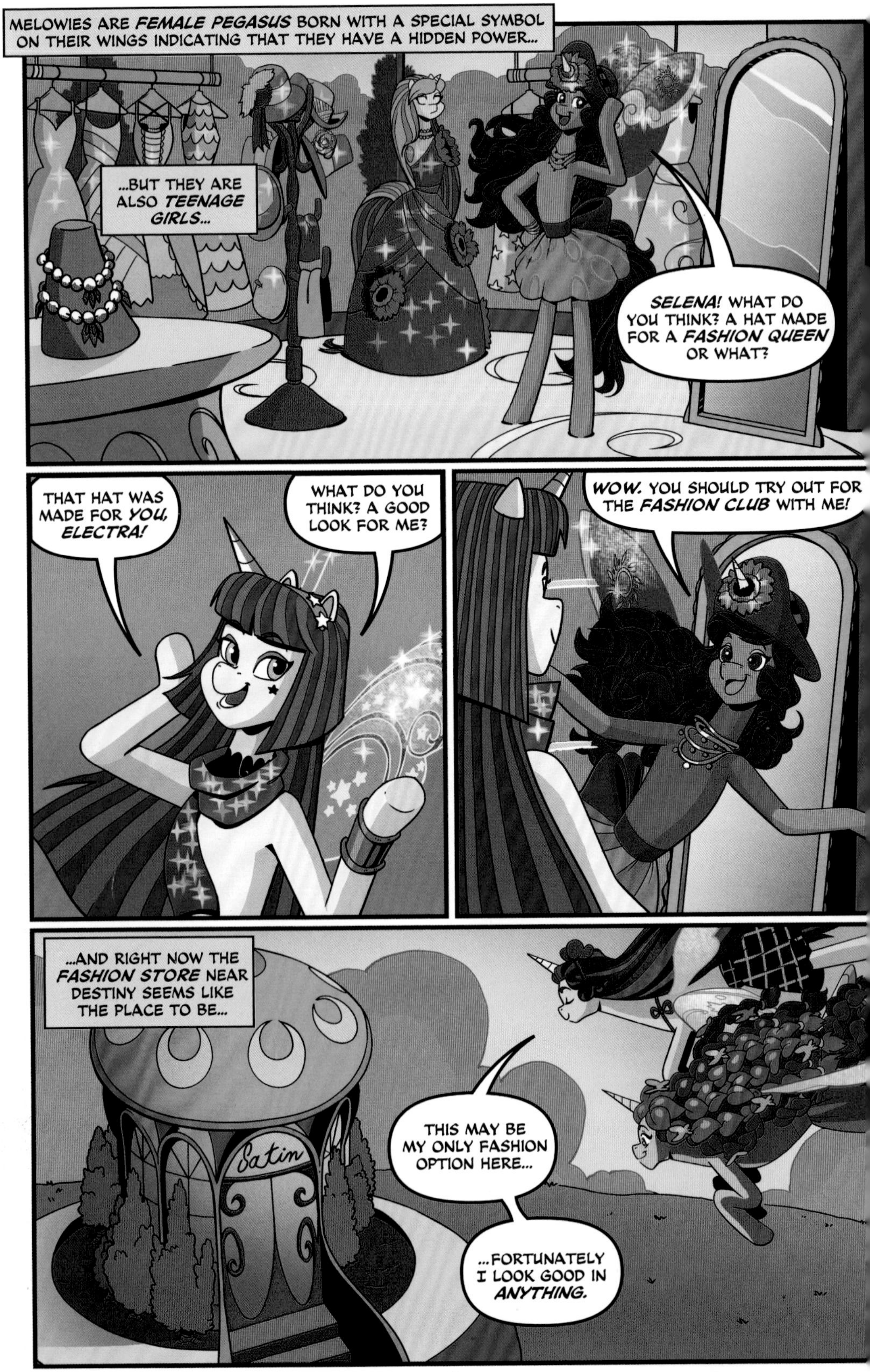
MELOWIES ARE FEMALE PEGASUS BORN WITH A SPECIAL SYMBOL ON THEIR WINGS INDICATING THAT THEY HAVE A HIDDEN POWER...
...BUT THEY ARE ALSO TEENAGE GIRLS...
SELENA! WHAT DO YOU THINK? A HAT MADE FOR A FASHION QUEEN OR WHAT?
THAT HAT WAS MADE FOR YOU, ELECTRA!
WHAT DO YOU THINK? A GOOD LOOK FOR ME?
WOW. YOU SHOULD TRY OUT FOR THE FASHION CLUB WITH ME!
...AND RIGHT NOW THE FASHION STORE NEAR DESTINY SEEMS LIKE THE PLACE TO BE...
Satin
THIS MAY BE MY ONLY FASHION OPTION HERE...
...FORTUNATELY I LOOK GOOD IN ANYTHING.

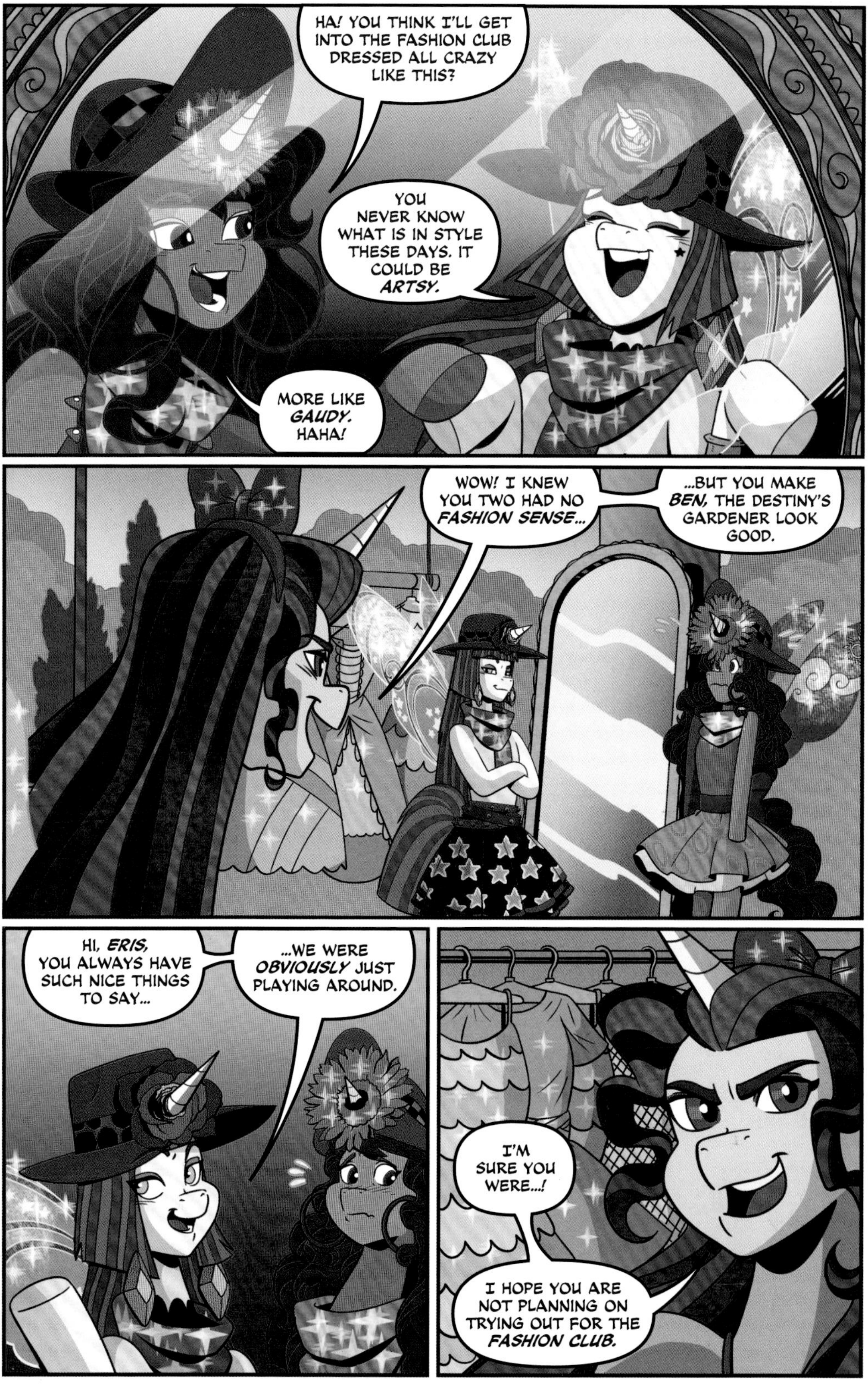
HA! YOU THINK I'LL GET INTO THE FASHION CLUB DRESSED ALL CRAZY LIKE THIS?
YOU NEVER KNOW WHAT IS IN STYLE THESE DAYS. IT COULD BE ARTSY.
MORE LIKE GAUDY. HAHA!
WOW! I KNEW YOU TWO HAD NO FASHION SENSE...
...BUT YOU MAKE BEN, THE DESTINY'S GARDENER LOOK GOOD.
HI, ERIS, YOU ALWAYS HAVE SUCH NICE THINGS TO SAY...
...WE WERE OBVIOUSLY JUST PLAYING AROUND.
I'M SURE YOU WERE...!
I HOPE YOU ARE NOT PLANNING ON TRYING OUT FOR THE FASHION CLUB.

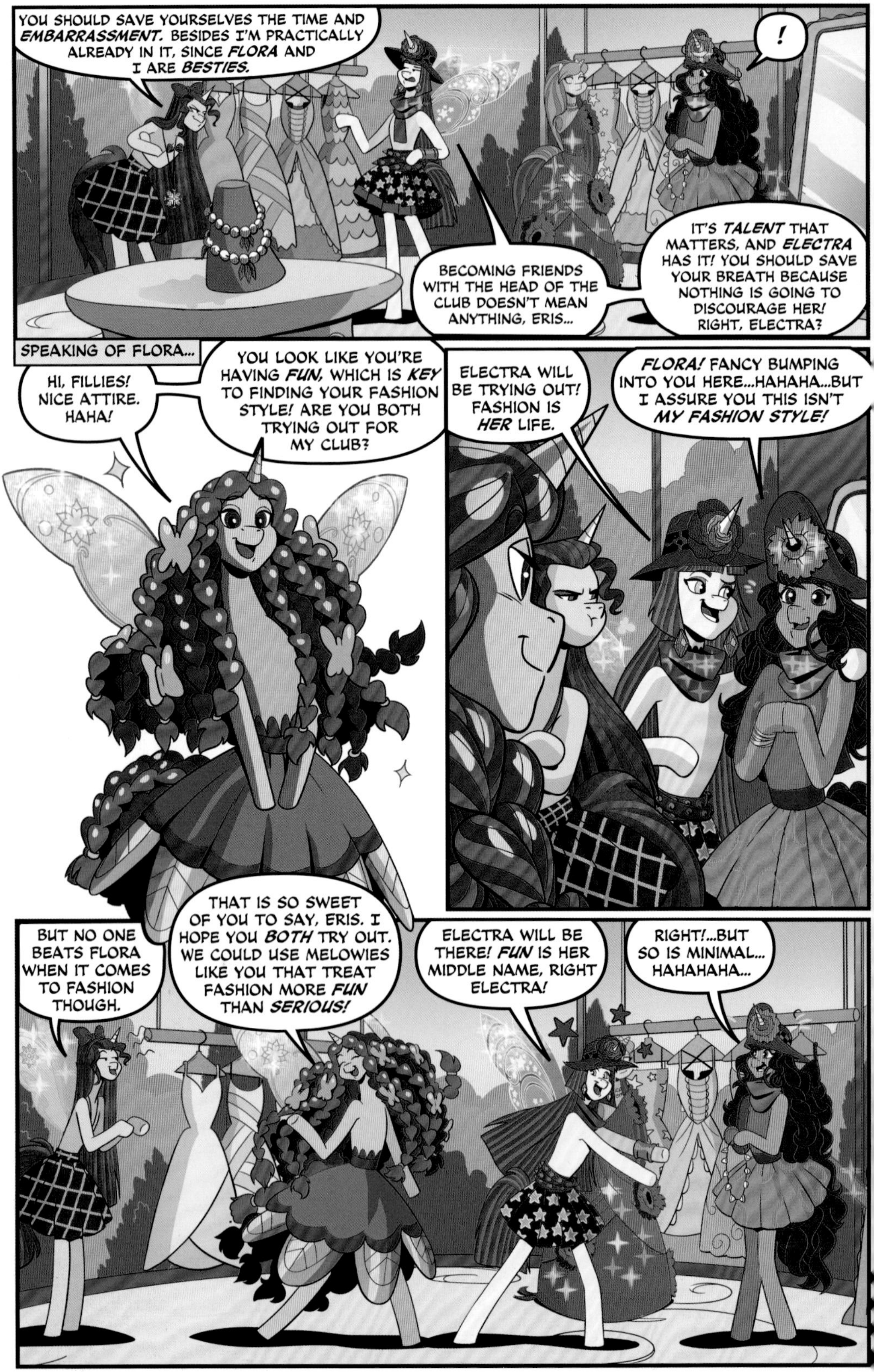
YOU SHOULD SAVE YOURSELVES THE TIME AND EMBARRASSMENT. BESIDES I'M PRACTICALLY ALREADY IN IT, SINCE FLORA AND I ARE BESTIES.
!
BECOMING FRIENDS WITH THE HEAD OF THE CLUB DOESN'T MEAN ANYTHING, ERIS...
IT'S TALENT THAT MATTERS, AND ELECTRA HAS IT! YOU SHOULD SAVE YOUR BREATH BECAUSE NOTHING IS GOING TO DISCOURAGE HER! RIGHT, ELECTRA?
SPEAKING OF FLORA...
HI, FILLIES! NICE ATTIRE. HAHA!
YOU LOOK LIKE YOU'RE HAVING FUN, WHICH IS KEY TO FINDING YOUR FASHION STYLE! ARE YOU BOTH TRYING OUT FOR MY CLUB?
FLORA! FANCY BUMPING INTO YOU HERE...HAHAHA...BUT I ASSURE YOU THIS ISN'T MY FASHION STYLE!
ELECTRA WILL BE TRYING OUT! FASHION IS HER LIFE.
BUT NO ONE BEATS FLORA WHEN IT COMES TO FASHION THOUGH.
THAT IS SO SWEET OF YOU TO SAY, ERIS. I HOPE YOU BOTH TRY OUT. WE COULD USE MELOWIES LIKE YOU THAT TREAT FASHION MORE FUN THAN SERIOUS!
ELECTRA WILL BE THERE! FUN IS HER MIDDLE NAME, RIGHT ELECTRA!
RIGHT!...BUT SO IS MINIMAL... HAHAHAHA...

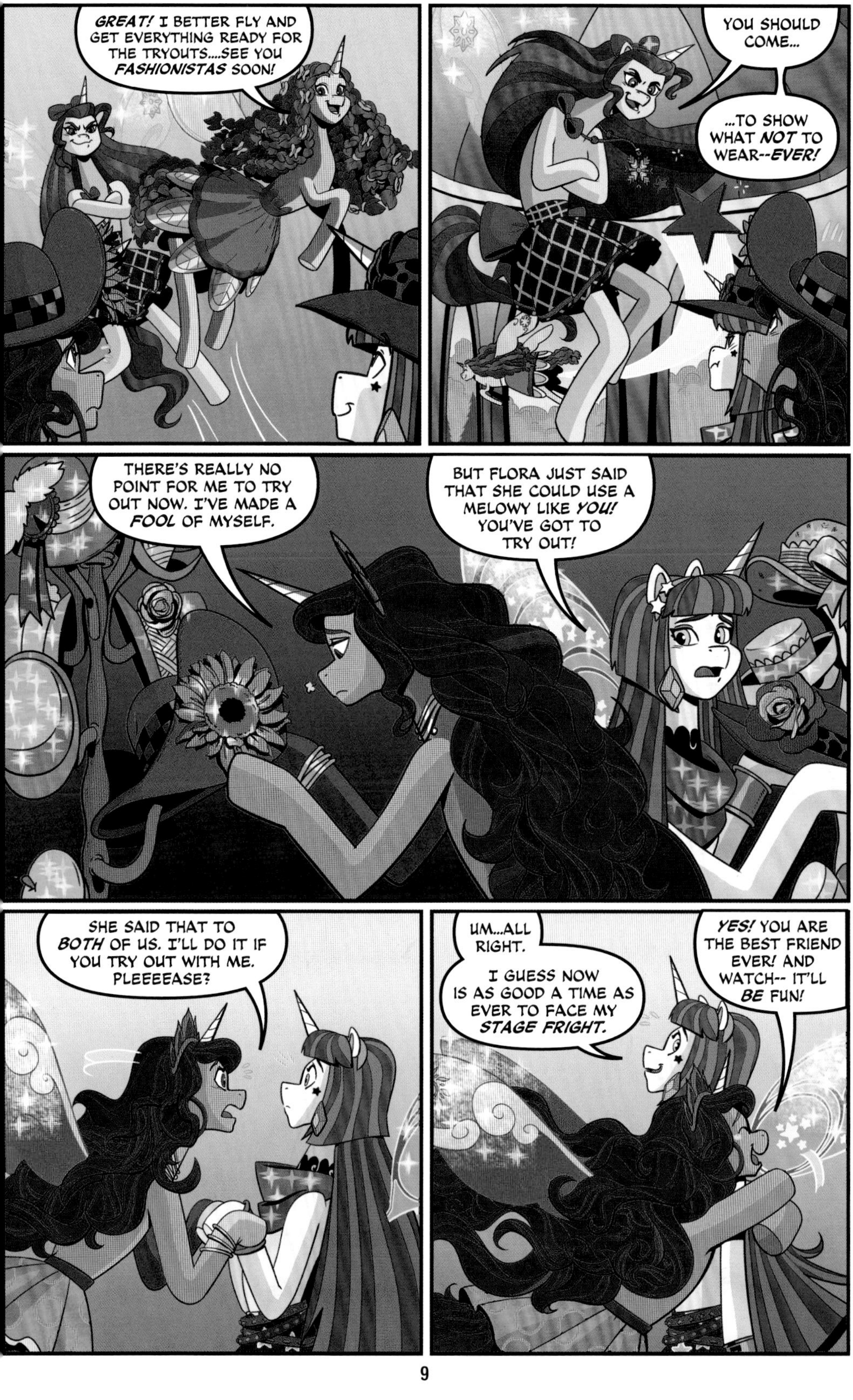
GREAT! I BETTER FLY AND GET EVERYTHING READY FOR THE TRYOUTS....SEE YOU FASHIONISTAS SOON!
YOU SHOULD COME...
...TO SHOW WHAT NOT TO WEAR--EVER!
THERE'S REALLY NO POINT FOR ME TO TRY OUT NOW. I'VE MADE A FOOL OF MYSELF.
BUT FLORA JUST SAID THAT SHE COULD USE A MELOWY LIKE YOU! YOU'VE GOT TO TRY OUT!
SHE SAID THAT TO BOTH OF US. I'LL DO IT IF YOU TRY OUT WITH ME. PLEEEEASE?
UM...ALL RIGHT.
I GUESS NOW IS AS GOOD A TIME AS EVER TO FACE MY STAGE FRIGHT.
YES! YOU ARE THE BEST FRIEND EVER! AND WATCH-- IT'LL BE FUN!

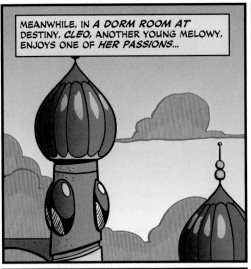

MEANWHILE, IN *A DORM ROOM AT DESTINY, CLEO,* ANOTHER YOUNG MELOWY, ENJOYS ONE OF *HER PASSIONS...*

...READING...

"...AND THE BABY DRAGON IS ALL ALONE IN THIS NEW STRANGE WORLD OF NO DRAGONS..." ≈GASP!≈

WOOF! WOOF!

FLUFFY! I'M TRYING TO READ!

HAHA! BUT I CAN'T BE MAD AT YOU-- YOU ARE SO SWEET!

I FEEL JUST LIKE THE *DRAGON* IN THIS BOOK...

A PART OF ME *STILL* CAN'T UNDERSTAND HOW I'M A MELOWY...

I DON'T HAVE A *SPECIAL SYMBOL* ON MY WINGS...

BUT *EVERYONE* SAYS I AM A MELOWY, SO I MUST BE...

...BUT HOW CAN I HAVE *MAGIC,* WITHOUT KNOWING WHICH *REALM* THAT I COME FROM?

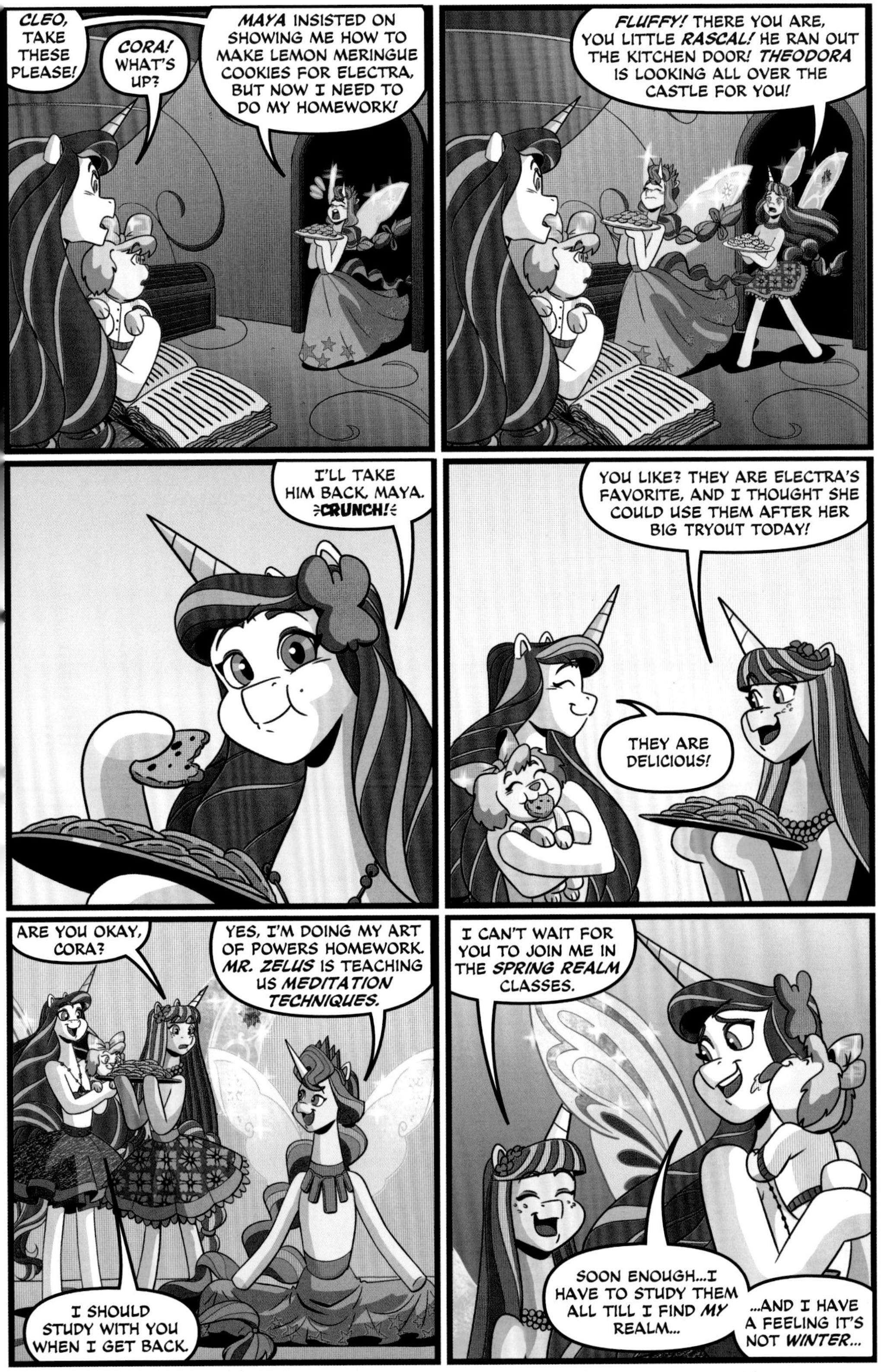
CLEO, TAKE THESE PLEASE!
CORA! WHAT'S UP?
MAYA INSISTED ON SHOWING ME HOW TO MAKE LEMON MERINGUE COOKIES FOR ELECTRA, BUT NOW I NEED TO DO MY HOMEWORK!
FLUFFY! THERE YOU ARE, YOU LITTLE RASCAL! HE RAN OUT THE KITCHEN DOOR! THEODORA IS LOOKING ALL OVER THE CASTLE FOR YOU!
I'LL TAKE HIM BACK, MAYA. CRUNCH!
YOU LIKE? THEY ARE ELECTRA'S FAVORITE, AND I THOUGHT SHE COULD USE THEM AFTER HER BIG TRYOUT TODAY!
THEY ARE DELICIOUS!
ARE YOU OKAY, CORA?
YES, I'M DOING MY ART OF POWERS HOMEWORK. MR. ZELUS IS TEACHING US MEDITATION TECHNIQUES.
I SHOULD STUDY WITH YOU WHEN I GET BACK.
I CAN'T WAIT FOR YOU TO JOIN ME IN THE SPRING REALM CLASSES.
SOON ENOUGH...I HAVE TO STUDY THEM ALL TILL I FIND MY REALM...
...AND I HAVE A FEELING IT'S NOT WINTER...

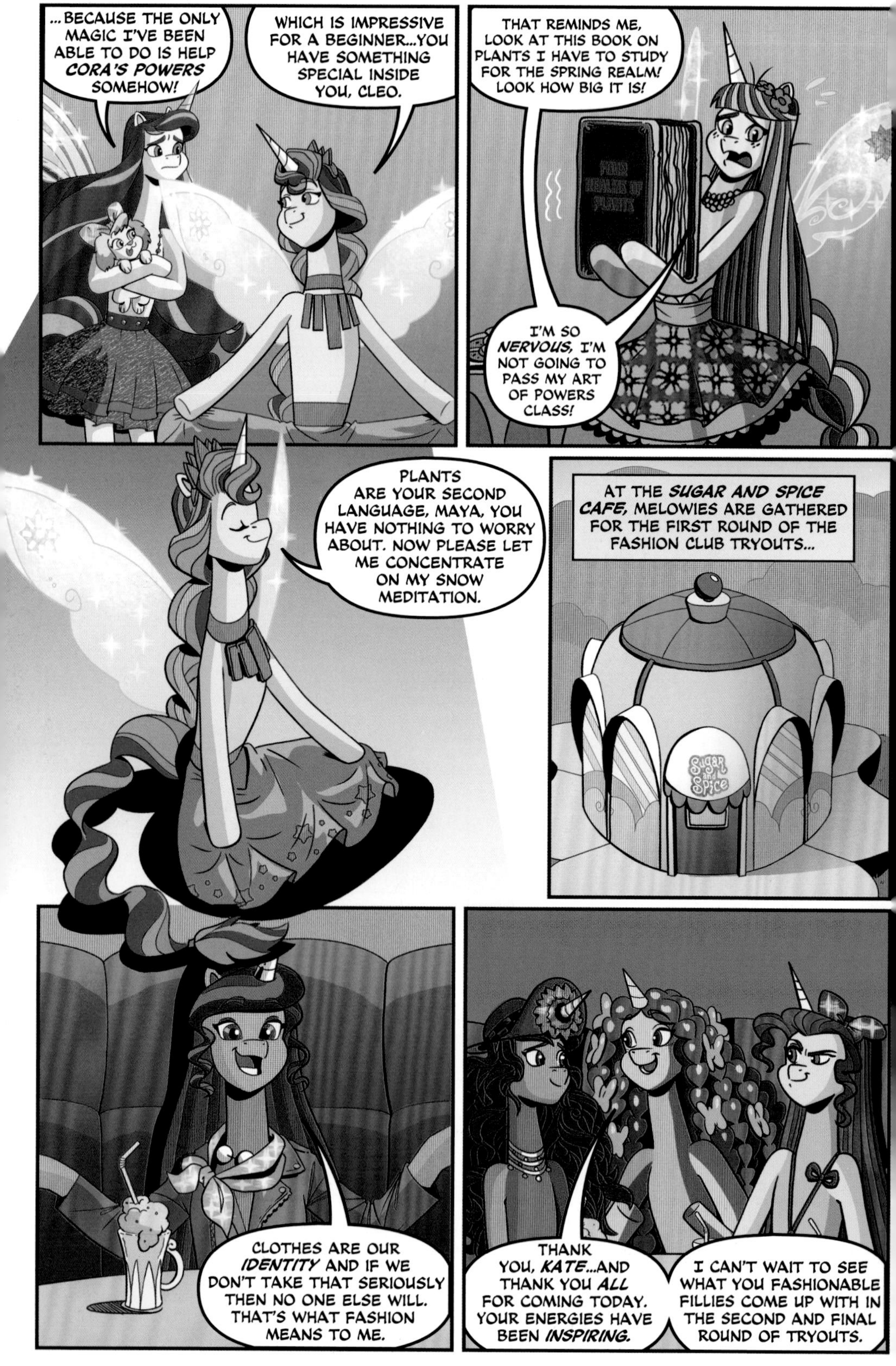
...BECAUSE THE ONLY MAGIC I'VE BEEN ABLE TO DO IS HELP *CORA'S POWERS* SOMEHOW!
WHICH IS IMPRESSIVE FOR A BEGINNER...YOU HAVE SOMETHING SPECIAL INSIDE YOU, CLEO.
THAT REMINDS ME, LOOK AT THIS BOOK ON PLANTS I HAVE TO STUDY FOR THE SPRING REALM! LOOK HOW BIG IT IS!
I'M SO *NERVOUS,* I'M NOT GOING TO PASS MY ART OF POWERS CLASS!
PLANTS ARE YOUR SECOND LANGUAGE, MAYA, YOU HAVE NOTHING TO WORRY ABOUT. NOW PLEASE LET ME CONCENTRATE ON MY SNOW MEDITATION.
AT THE *SUGAR AND SPICE CAFE,* MELOWIES ARE GATHERED FOR THE FIRST ROUND OF THE FASHION CLUB TRYOUTS...
Sugar and Spice
CLOTHES ARE OUR *IDENTITY* AND IF WE DON'T TAKE THAT SERIOUSLY THEN NO ONE ELSE WILL. THAT'S WHAT FASHION MEANS TO ME.
THANK YOU, *KATE*...AND THANK YOU *ALL* FOR COMING TODAY. YOUR ENERGIES HAVE BEEN *INSPIRING.*
I CAN'T WAIT TO SEE WHAT YOU FASHIONABLE FILLIES COME UP WITH IN THE SECOND AND FINAL ROUND OF TRYOUTS.

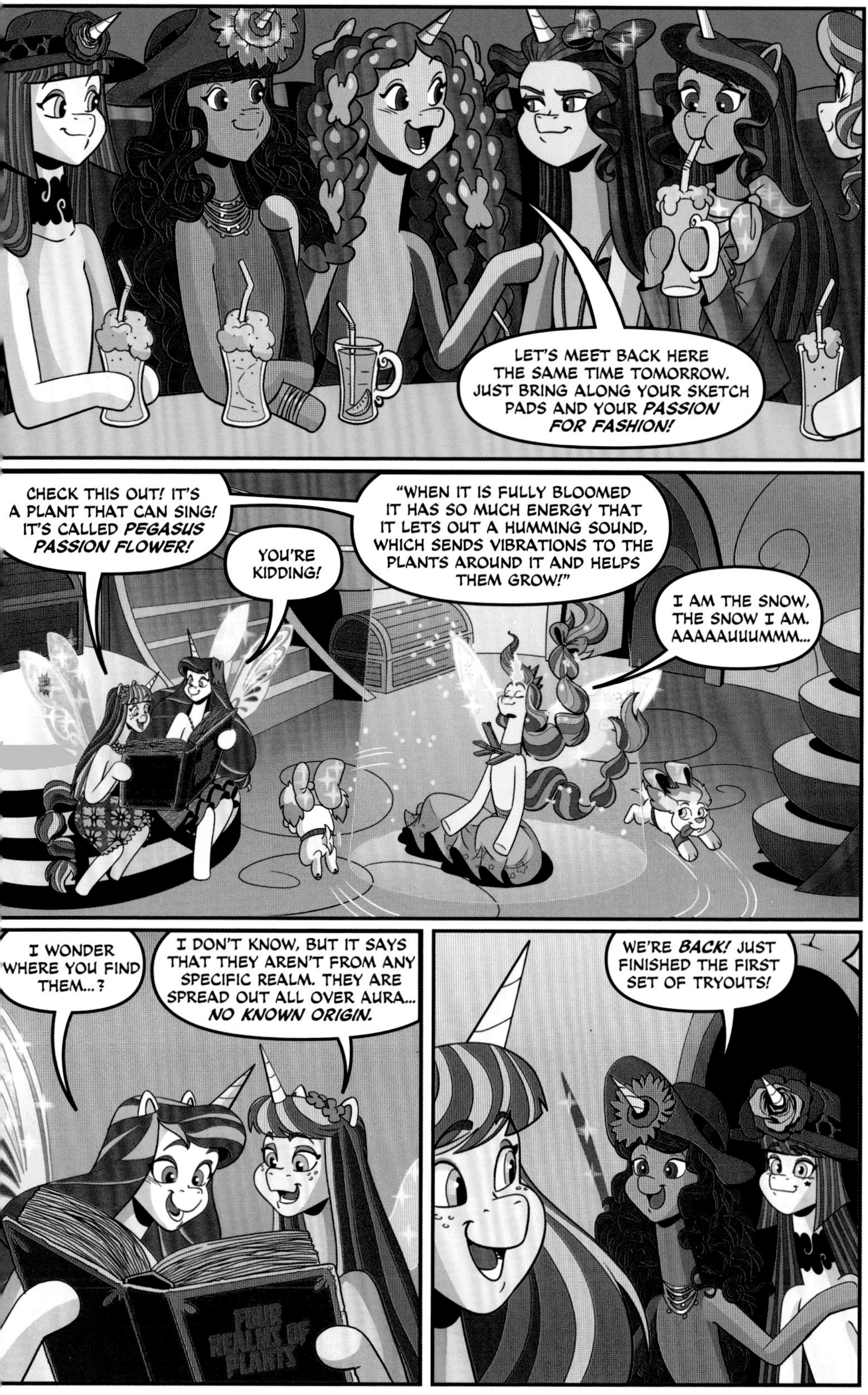
LET'S MEET BACK HERE THE SAME TIME TOMORROW. JUST BRING ALONG YOUR SKETCH PADS AND YOUR *PASSION FOR FASHION!*
CHECK THIS OUT! IT'S A PLANT THAT CAN SING! IT'S CALLED *PEGASUS PASSION FLOWER!*
YOU'RE KIDDING!
"WHEN IT IS FULLY BLOOMED IT HAS SO MUCH ENERGY THAT IT LETS OUT A HUMMING SOUND, WHICH SENDS VIBRATIONS TO THE PLANTS AROUND IT AND HELPS THEM GROW!"
I AM THE SNOW, THE SNOW I AM. AAAAAUUUMMM...
I WONDER WHERE YOU FIND THEM...?
I DON'T KNOW, BUT IT SAYS THAT THEY AREN'T FROM ANY SPECIFIC REALM. THEY ARE SPREAD OUT ALL OVER AURA... *NO KNOWN ORIGIN.*
FOUR REALMS OF PLANTS
WE'RE *BACK!* JUST FINISHED THE FIRST SET OF TRYOUTS!

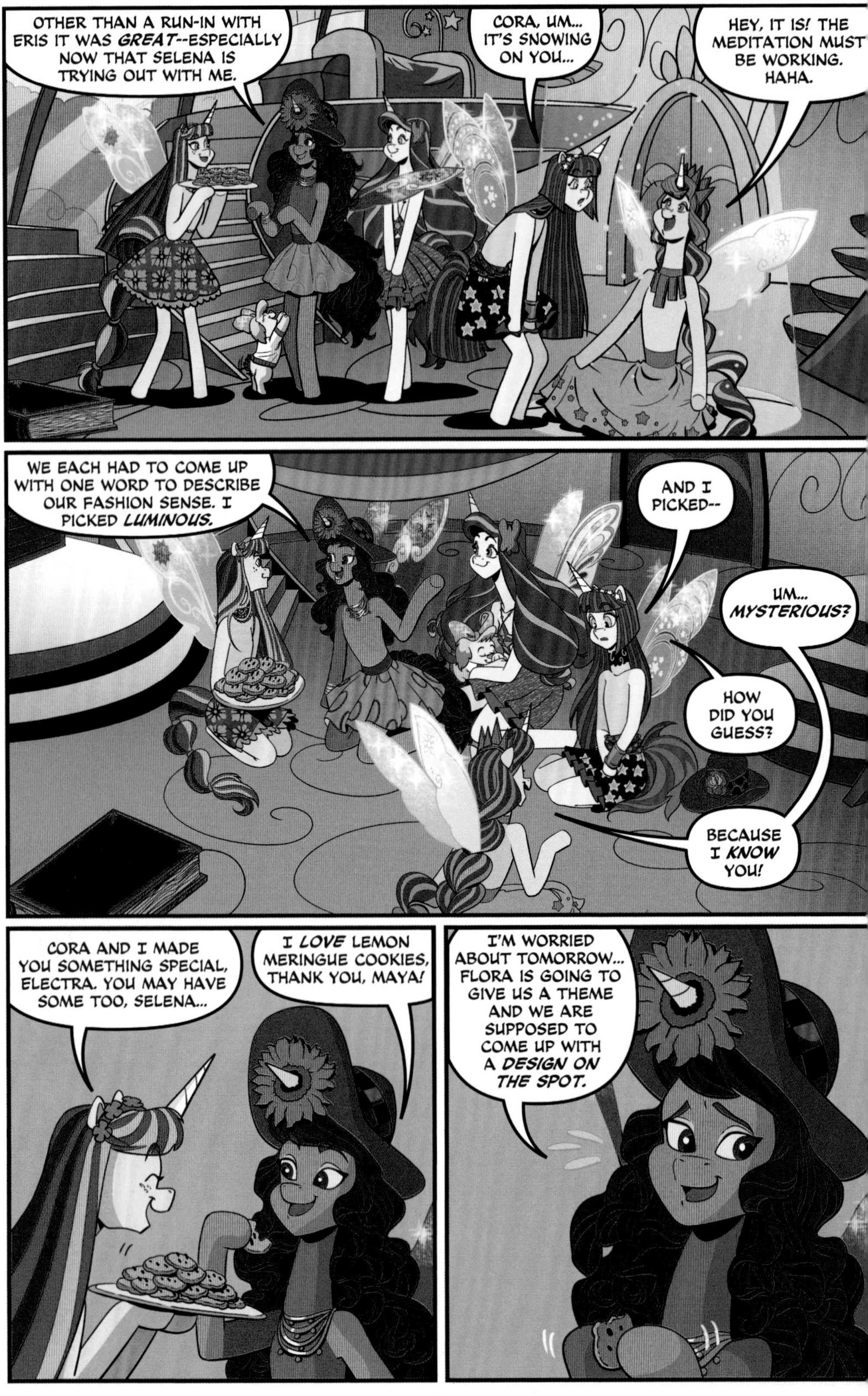
OTHER THAN A RUN-IN WITH ERIS IT WAS GREAT--ESPECIALLY NOW THAT SELENA IS TRYING OUT WITH ME.
CORA, UM... IT'S SNOWING ON YOU...
HEY, IT IS! THE MEDITATION MUST BE WORKING. HAHA.
WE EACH HAD TO COME UP WITH ONE WORD TO DESCRIBE OUR FASHION SENSE. I PICKED LUMINOUS.
AND I PICKED--
UM... MYSTERIOUS?
HOW DID YOU GUESS?
BECAUSE I KNOW YOU!
CORA AND I MADE YOU SOMETHING SPECIAL, ELECTRA. YOU MAY HAVE SOME TOO, SELENA...
I LOVE LEMON MERINGUE COOKIES, THANK YOU, MAYA!
I'M WORRIED ABOUT TOMORROW... FLORA IS GOING TO GIVE US A THEME AND WE ARE SUPPOSED TO COME UP WITH A DESIGN ON THE SPOT.

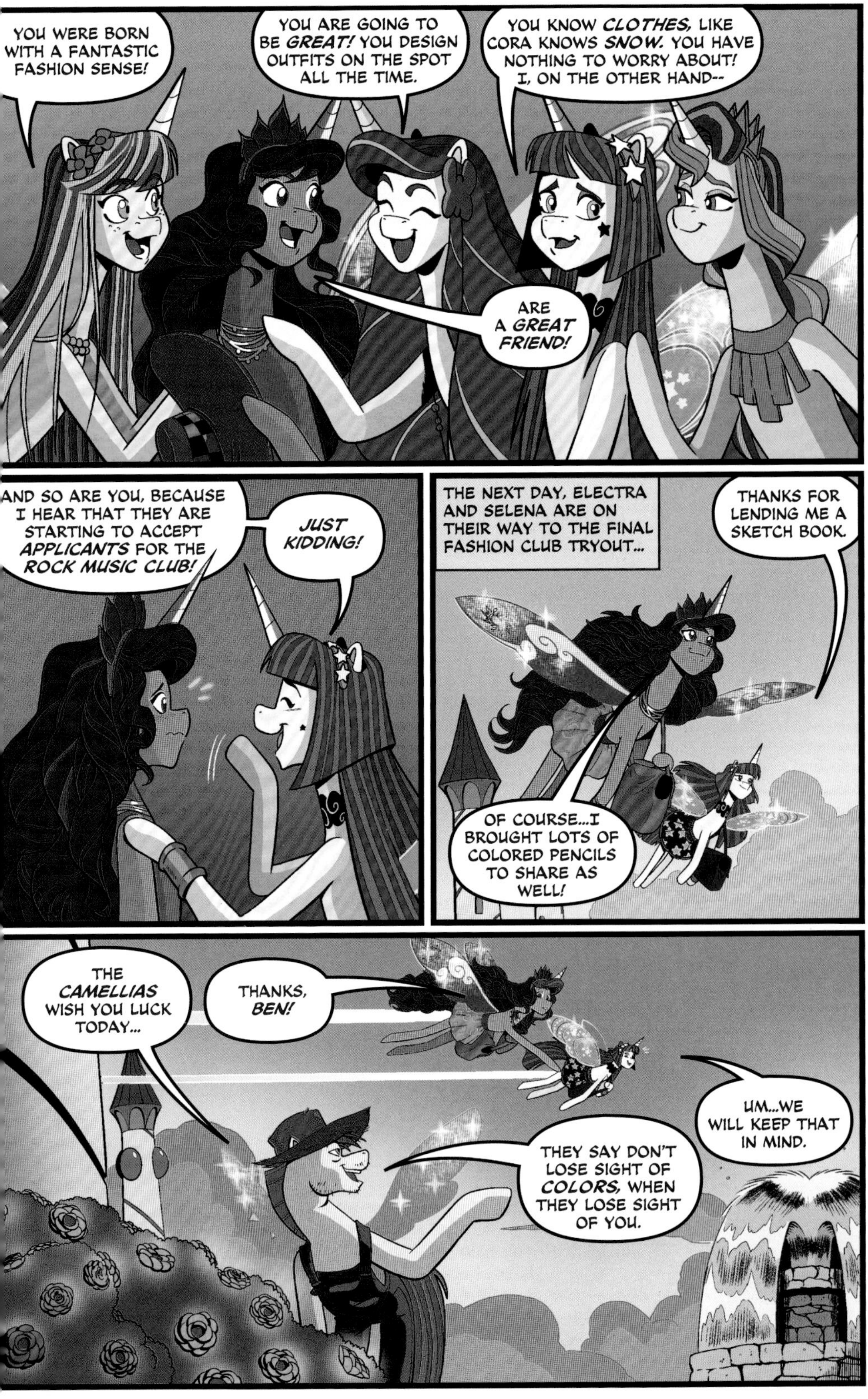

YOU WERE BORN WITH A FANTASTIC FASHION SENSE!
YOU ARE GOING TO BE *GREAT!* YOU DESIGN OUTFITS ON THE SPOT ALL THE TIME.
YOU KNOW *CLOTHES,* LIKE CORA KNOWS *SNOW.* YOU HAVE NOTHING TO WORRY ABOUT! I, ON THE OTHER HAND--
ARE A *GREAT FRIEND!*
AND SO ARE YOU, BECAUSE I HEAR THAT THEY ARE STARTING TO ACCEPT *APPLICANTS* FOR THE *ROCK MUSIC CLUB!*
JUST KIDDING!
THE NEXT DAY, ELECTRA AND SELENA ARE ON THEIR WAY TO THE FINAL FASHION CLUB TRYOUT...
THANKS FOR LENDING ME A SKETCH BOOK.
OF COURSE...I BROUGHT LOTS OF COLORED PENCILS TO SHARE AS WELL!
THE *CAMELLIAS* WISH YOU LUCK TODAY...
THANKS, *BEN!*
THEY SAY DON'T LOSE SIGHT OF *COLORS,* WHEN THEY LOSE SIGHT OF YOU.
UM...WE WILL KEEP THAT IN MIND.

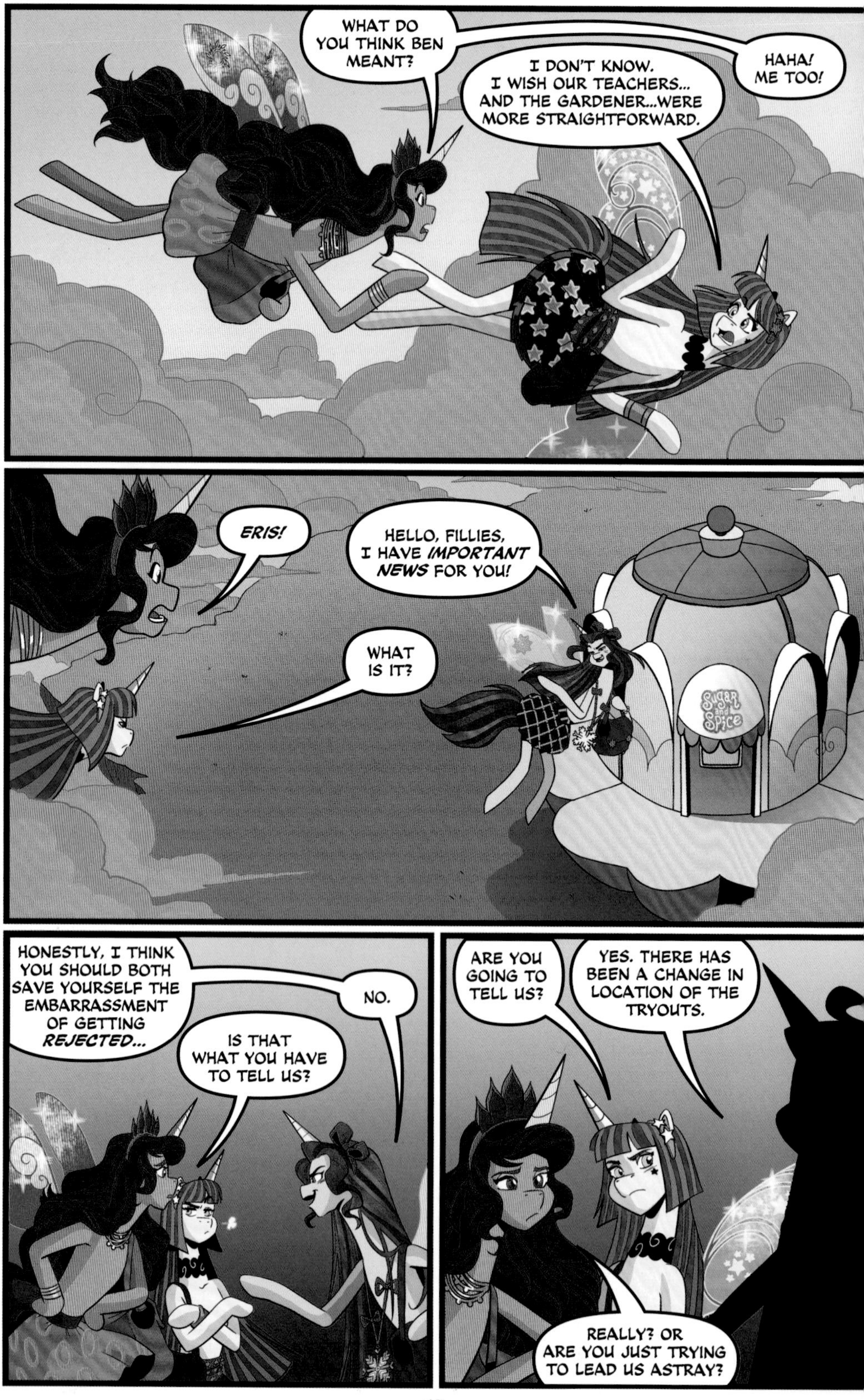
WHAT DO YOU THINK BEN MEANT?
I DON'T KNOW. I WISH OUR TEACHERS... AND THE GARDENER...WERE MORE STRAIGHTFORWARD.
HAHA! ME TOO!
ERIS!
HELLO, FILLIES, I HAVE IMPORTANT NEWS FOR YOU!
WHAT IS IT?
SUGAR and SPICE
HONESTLY, I THINK YOU SHOULD BOTH SAVE YOURSELF THE EMBARRASSMENT OF GETTING REJECTED...
NO.
IS THAT WHAT YOU HAVE TO TELL US?
ARE YOU GOING TO TELL US?
YES. THERE HAS BEEN A CHANGE IN LOCATION OF THE TRYOUTS.
REALLY? OR ARE YOU JUST TRYING TO LEAD US ASTRAY?

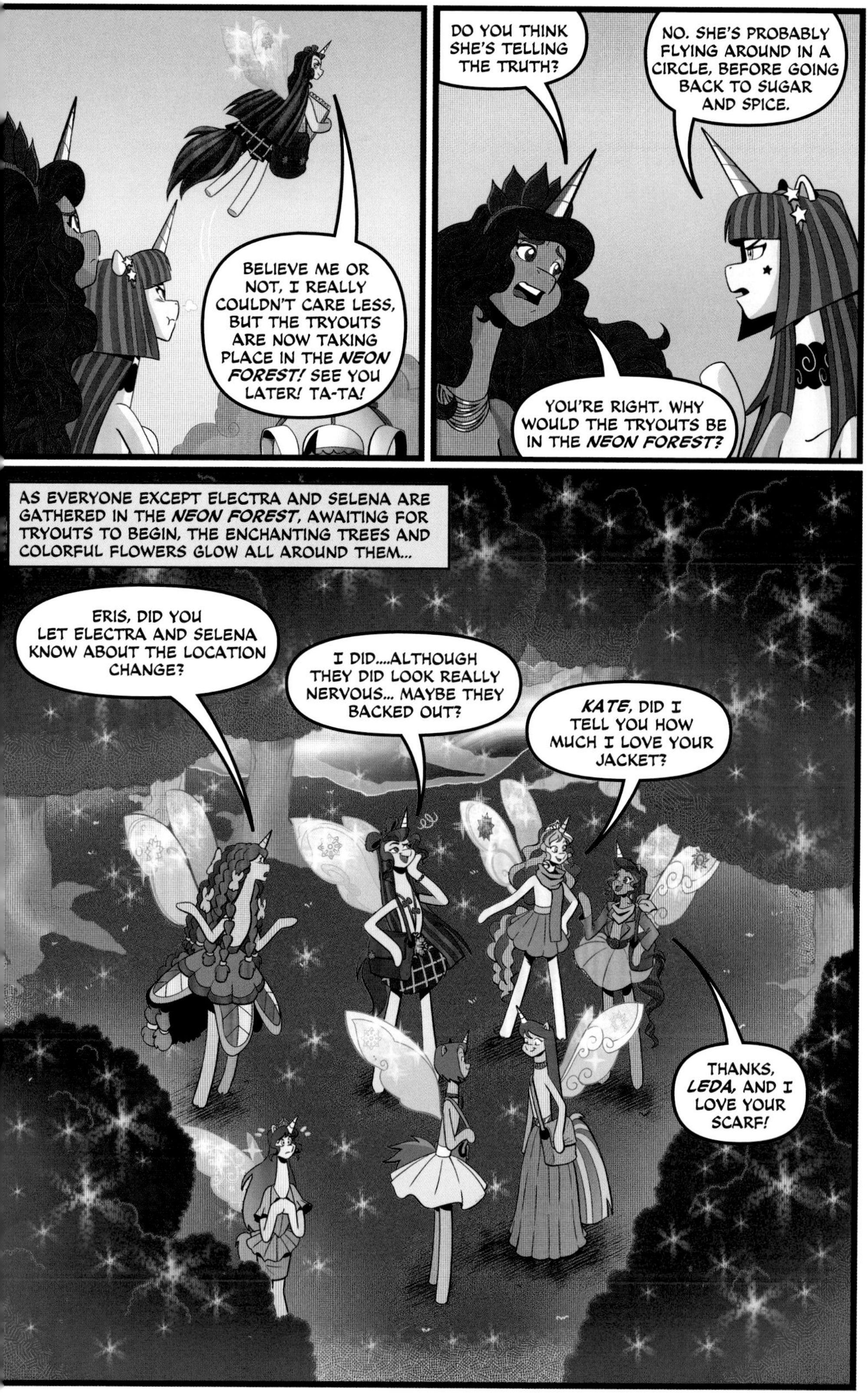
BELIEVE ME OR NOT, I REALLY COULDN'T CARE LESS, BUT THE TRYOUTS ARE NOW TAKING PLACE IN THE *NEON FOREST!* SEE YOU LATER! TA-TA!
DO YOU THINK SHE'S TELLING THE TRUTH?
NO. SHE'S PROBABLY FLYING AROUND IN A CIRCLE, BEFORE GOING BACK TO SUGAR AND SPICE.
YOU'RE RIGHT. WHY WOULD THE TRYOUTS BE IN THE *NEON FOREST?*
AS EVERYONE EXCEPT ELECTRA AND SELENA ARE GATHERED IN THE *NEON FOREST*, AWAITING FOR TRYOUTS TO BEGIN, THE ENCHANTING TREES AND COLORFUL FLOWERS GLOW ALL AROUND THEM...
ERIS, DID YOU LET ELECTRA AND SELENA KNOW ABOUT THE LOCATION CHANGE?
I DID....ALTHOUGH THEY DID LOOK REALLY NERVOUS... MAYBE THEY BACKED OUT?
KATE, DID I TELL YOU HOW MUCH I LOVE YOUR JACKET?
THANKS, *LEDA*, AND I LOVE YOUR SCARF!

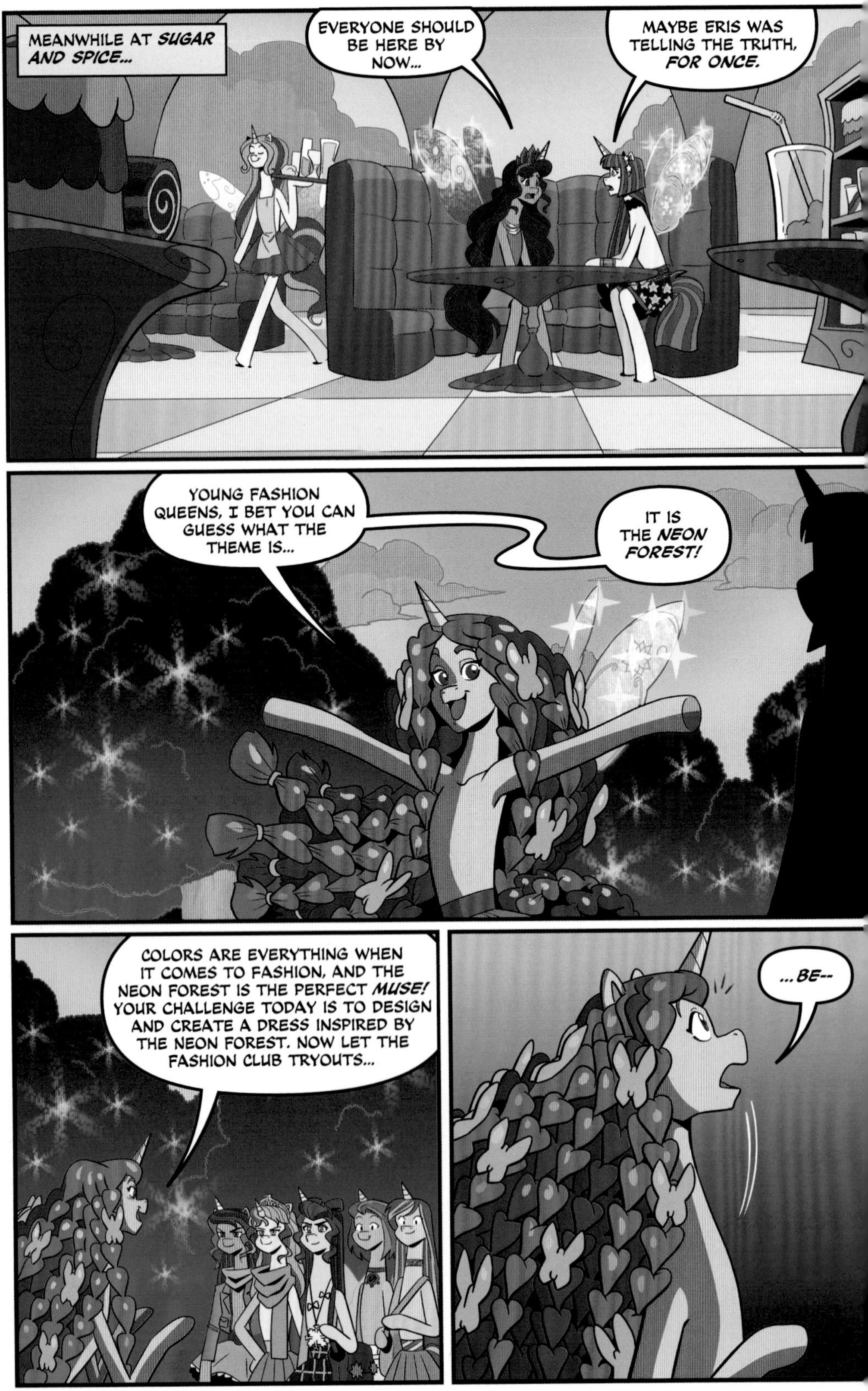
MEANWHILE AT SUGAR AND SPICE...
EVERYONE SHOULD BE HERE BY NOW...
MAYBE ERIS WAS TELLING THE TRUTH, FOR ONCE.
YOUNG FASHION QUEENS, I BET YOU CAN GUESS WHAT THE THEME IS...
IT IS THE NEON FOREST!
COLORS ARE EVERYTHING WHEN IT COMES TO FASHION, AND THE NEON FOREST IS THE PERFECT MUSE! YOUR CHALLENGE TODAY IS TO DESIGN AND CREATE A DRESS INSPIRED BY THE NEON FOREST. NOW LET THE FASHION CLUB TRYOUTS...
...BE--

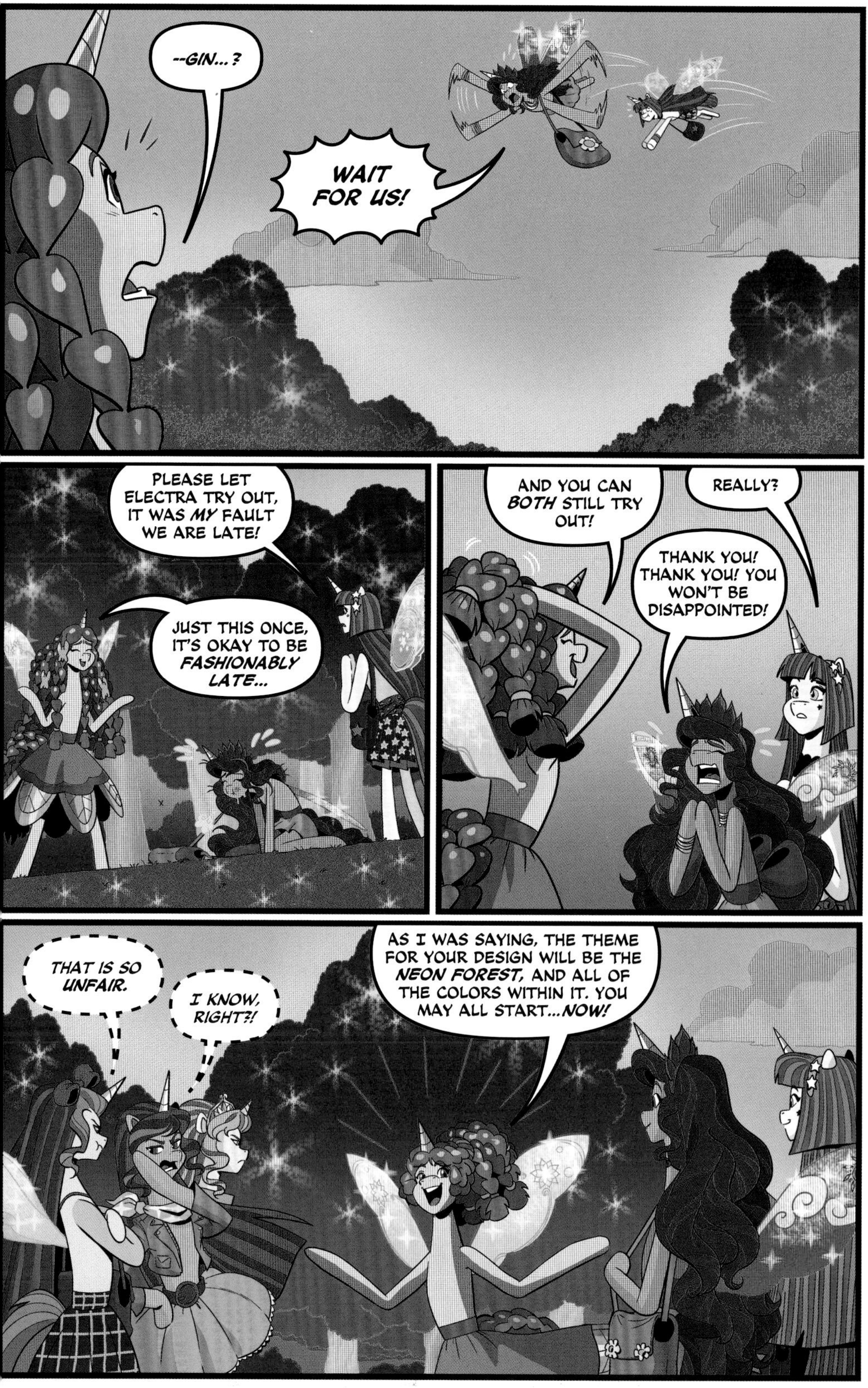
--GIN...?
WAIT FOR US!
PLEASE LET ELECTRA TRY OUT, IT WAS MY FAULT WE ARE LATE!
JUST THIS ONCE, IT'S OKAY TO BE FASHIONABLY LATE...
AND YOU CAN BOTH STILL TRY OUT!
REALLY?
THANK YOU! THANK YOU! YOU WON'T BE DISAPPOINTED!
THAT IS SO UNFAIR.
I KNOW, RIGHT?!
AS I WAS SAYING, THE THEME FOR YOUR DESIGN WILL BE THE NEON FOREST, AND ALL OF THE COLORS WITHIN IT. YOU MAY ALL START...NOW!

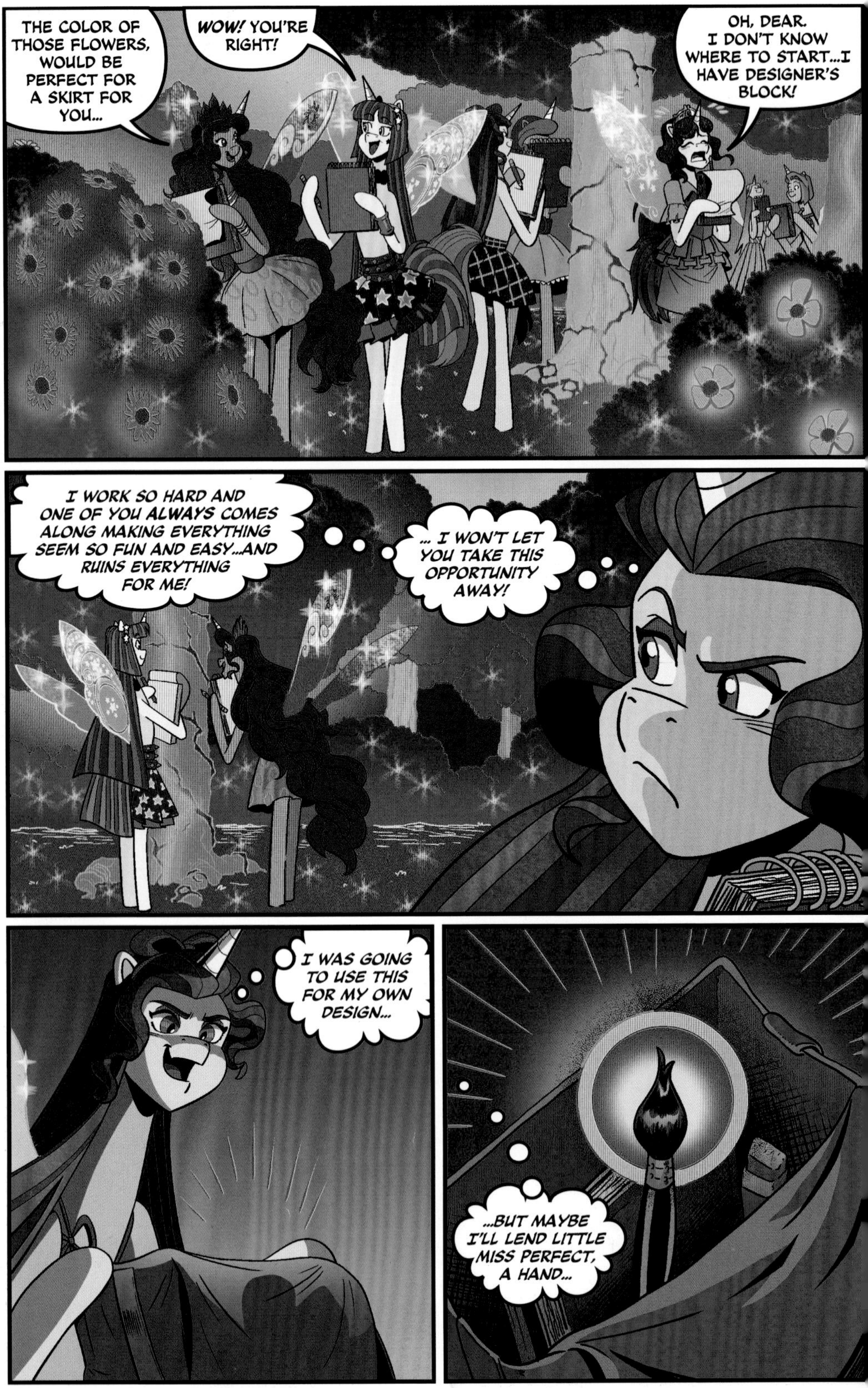

THE COLOR OF THOSE FLOWERS, WOULD BE PERFECT FOR A SKIRT FOR YOU...
WOW! YOU'RE RIGHT!
OH, DEAR. I DON'T KNOW WHERE TO START...I HAVE DESIGNER'S BLOCK!
I WORK SO HARD AND ONE OF YOU ALWAYS COMES ALONG MAKING EVERYTHING SEEM SO FUN AND EASY...AND RUINS EVERYTHING FOR ME!
... I WON'T LET YOU TAKE THIS OPPORTUNITY AWAY!
I WAS GOING TO USE THIS FOR MY OWN DESIGN...
...BUT MAYBE I'LL LEND LITTLE MISS PERFECT, A HAND...

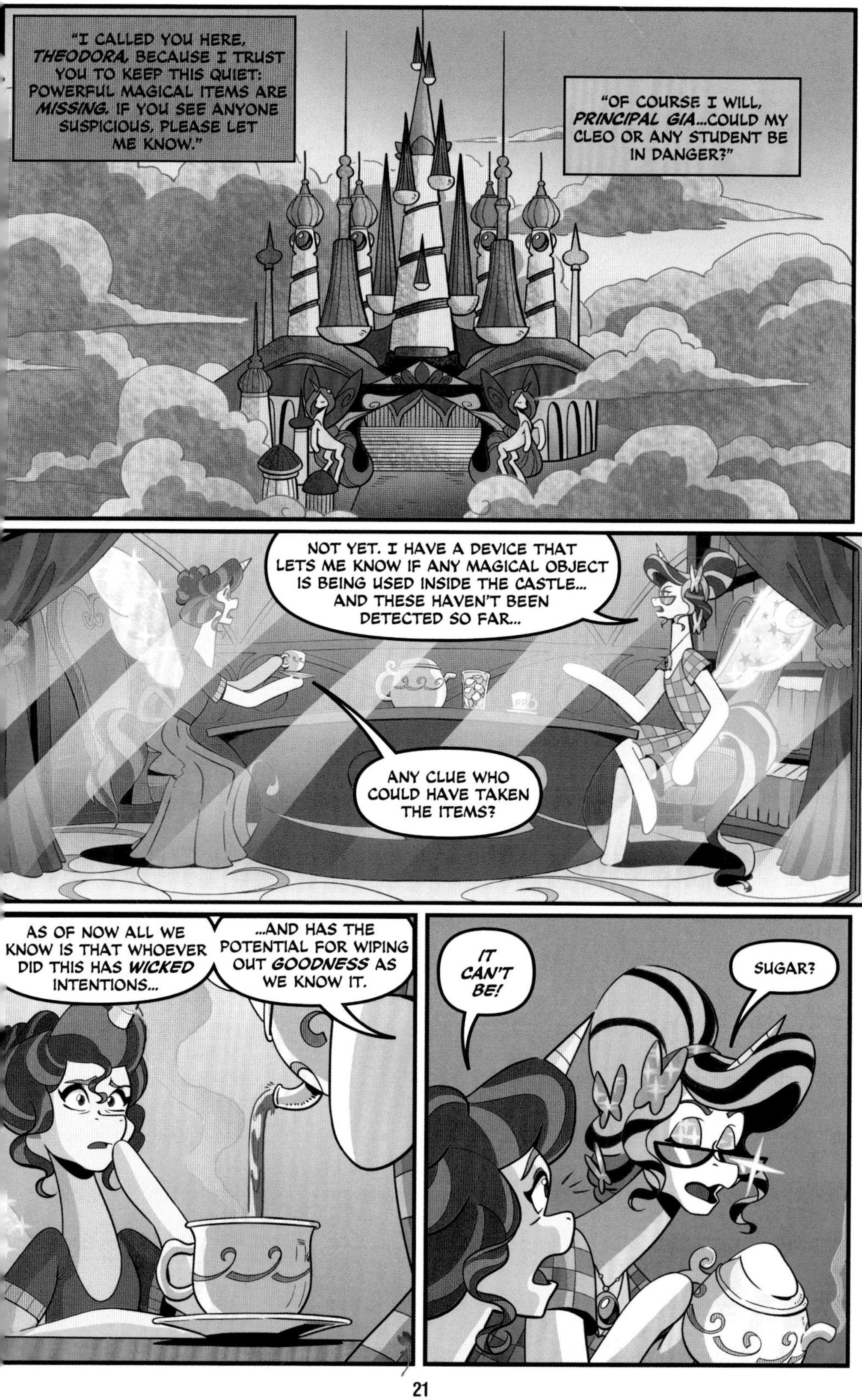
"I CALLED YOU HERE, THEODORA, BECAUSE I TRUST YOU TO KEEP THIS QUIET: POWERFUL MAGICAL ITEMS ARE MISSING. IF YOU SEE ANYONE SUSPICIOUS, PLEASE LET ME KNOW."
"OF COURSE I WILL, PRINCIPAL GIA...COULD MY CLEO OR ANY STUDENT BE IN DANGER?"
NOT YET. I HAVE A DEVICE THAT LETS ME KNOW IF ANY MAGICAL OBJECT IS BEING USED INSIDE THE CASTLE... AND THESE HAVEN'T BEEN DETECTED SO FAR...
ANY CLUE WHO COULD HAVE TAKEN THE ITEMS?
AS OF NOW ALL WE KNOW IS THAT WHOEVER DID THIS HAS WICKED INTENTIONS...
...AND HAS THE POTENTIAL FOR WIPING OUT GOODNESS AS WE KNOW IT.
IT CAN'T BE!
SUGAR?

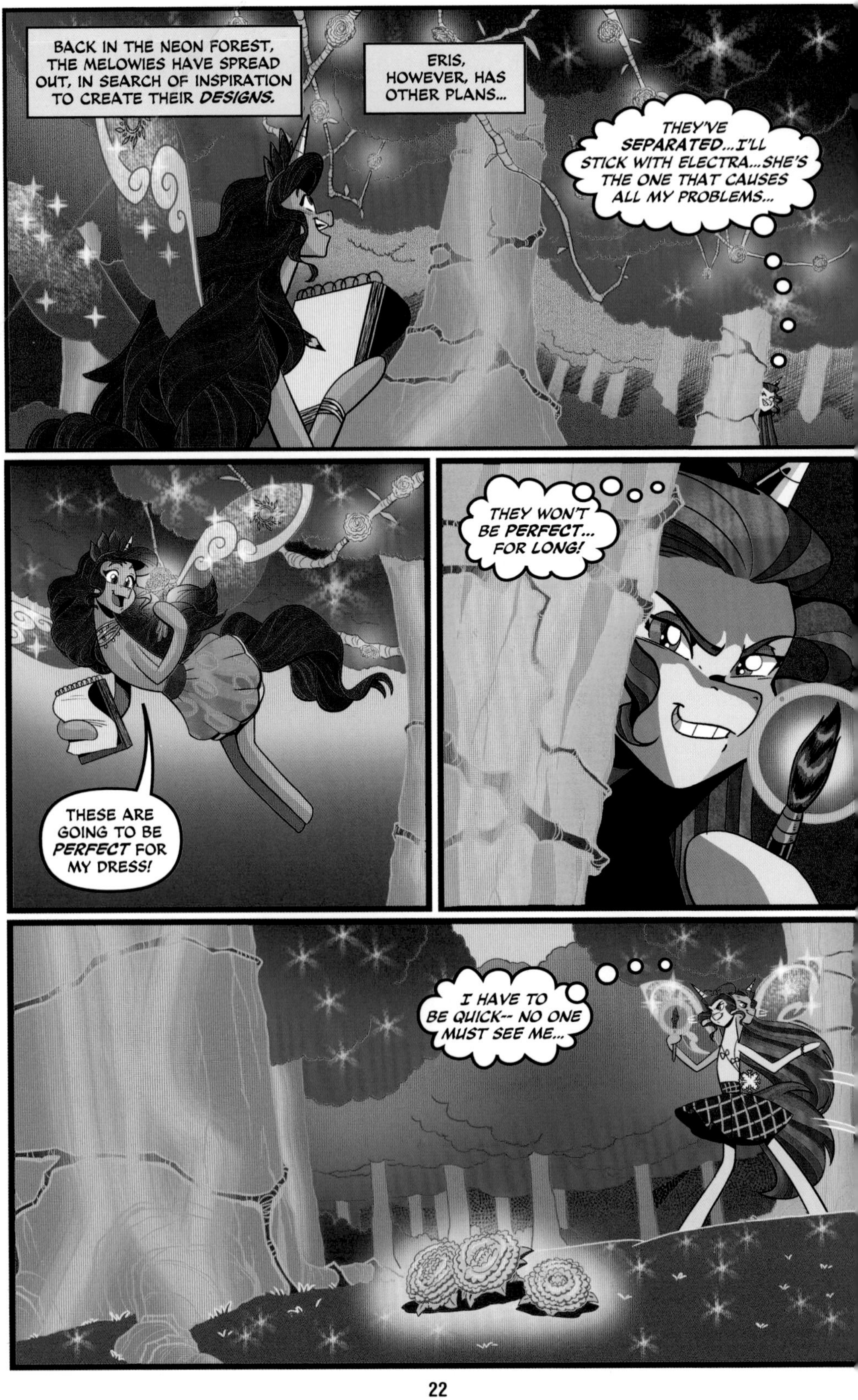
BACK IN THE NEON FOREST, THE MELOWIES HAVE SPREAD OUT, IN SEARCH OF INSPIRATION TO CREATE THEIR *DESIGNS.*
ERIS, HOWEVER, HAS OTHER PLANS...
THEY'VE *SEPARATED*...I'LL STICK WITH ELECTRA...SHE'S THE ONE THAT CAUSES ALL MY PROBLEMS...
THESE ARE GOING TO BE *PERFECT* FOR MY DRESS!
THEY WON'T BE *PERFECT*... FOR LONG!
I HAVE TO BE QUICK-- NO ONE MUST SEE ME...

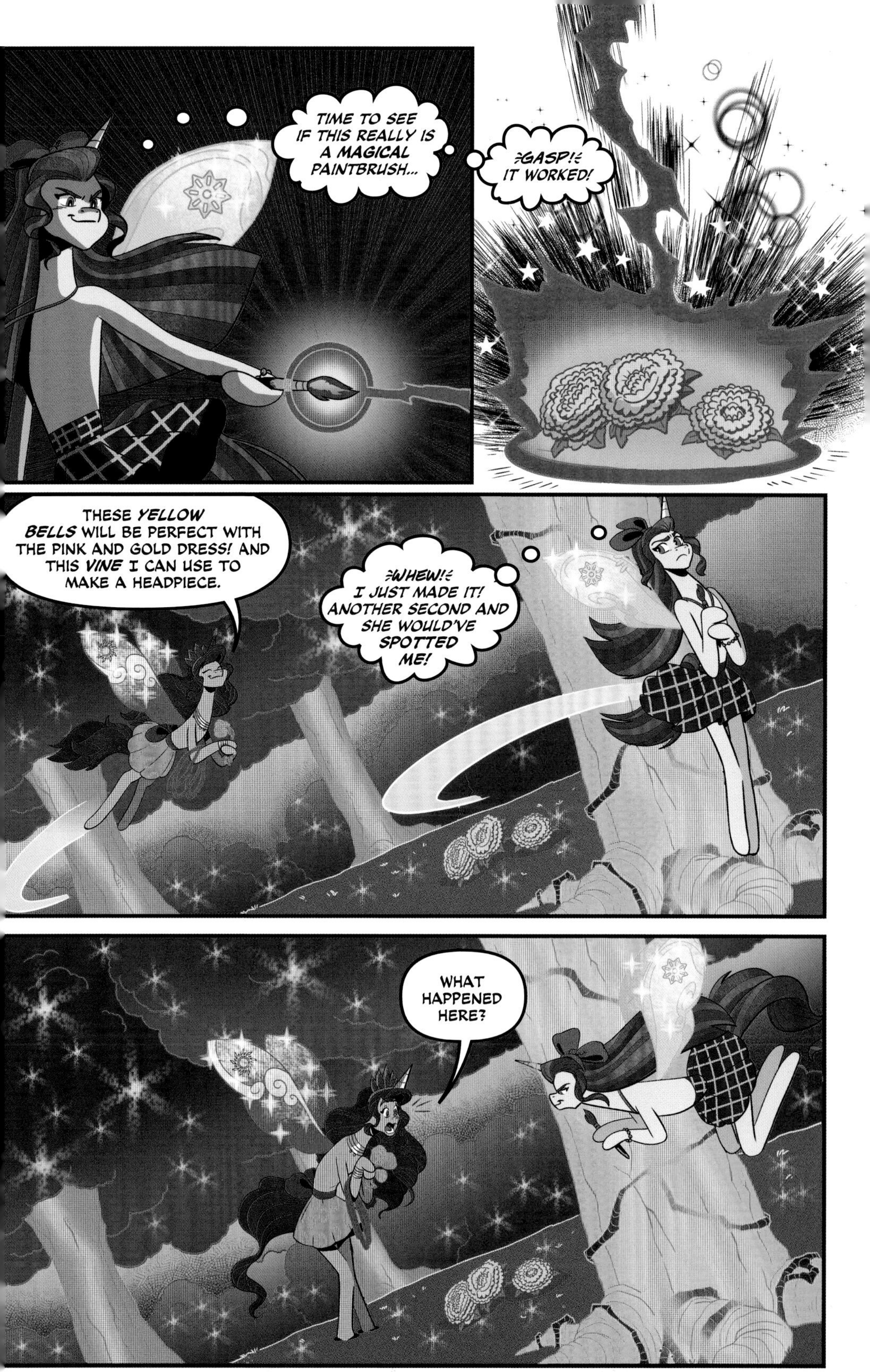
TIME TO SEE IF THIS REALLY IS A MAGICAL PAINTBRUSH...
GASP! IT WORKED!
THESE YELLOW BELLS WILL BE PERFECT WITH THE PINK AND GOLD DRESS! AND THIS VINE I CAN USE TO MAKE A HEADPIECE.
WHEW! I JUST MADE IT! ANOTHER SECOND AND SHE WOULD'VE SPOTTED ME!
WHAT HAPPENED HERE?

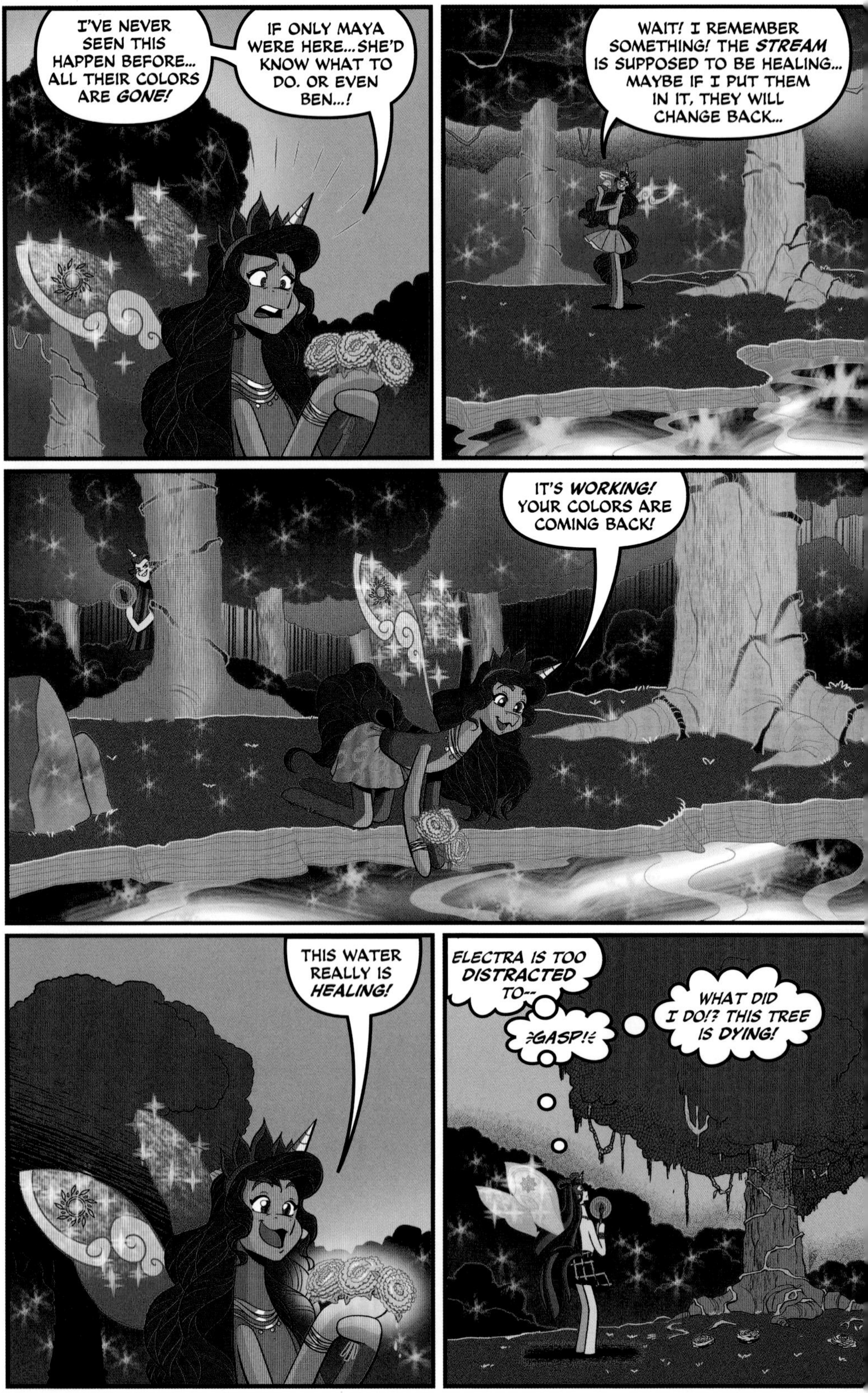
I'VE NEVER SEEN THIS HAPPEN BEFORE... ALL THEIR COLORS ARE GONE!
IF ONLY MAYA WERE HERE...SHE'D KNOW WHAT TO DO. OR EVEN BEN...!
WAIT! I REMEMBER SOMETHING! THE STREAM IS SUPPOSED TO BE HEALING... MAYBE IF I PUT THEM IN IT, THEY WILL CHANGE BACK...
IT'S WORKING! YOUR COLORS ARE COMING BACK!
THIS WATER REALLY IS HEALING!
ELECTRA IS TOO DISTRACTED TO--
GASP!
WHAT DID I DO!? THIS TREE IS DYING!

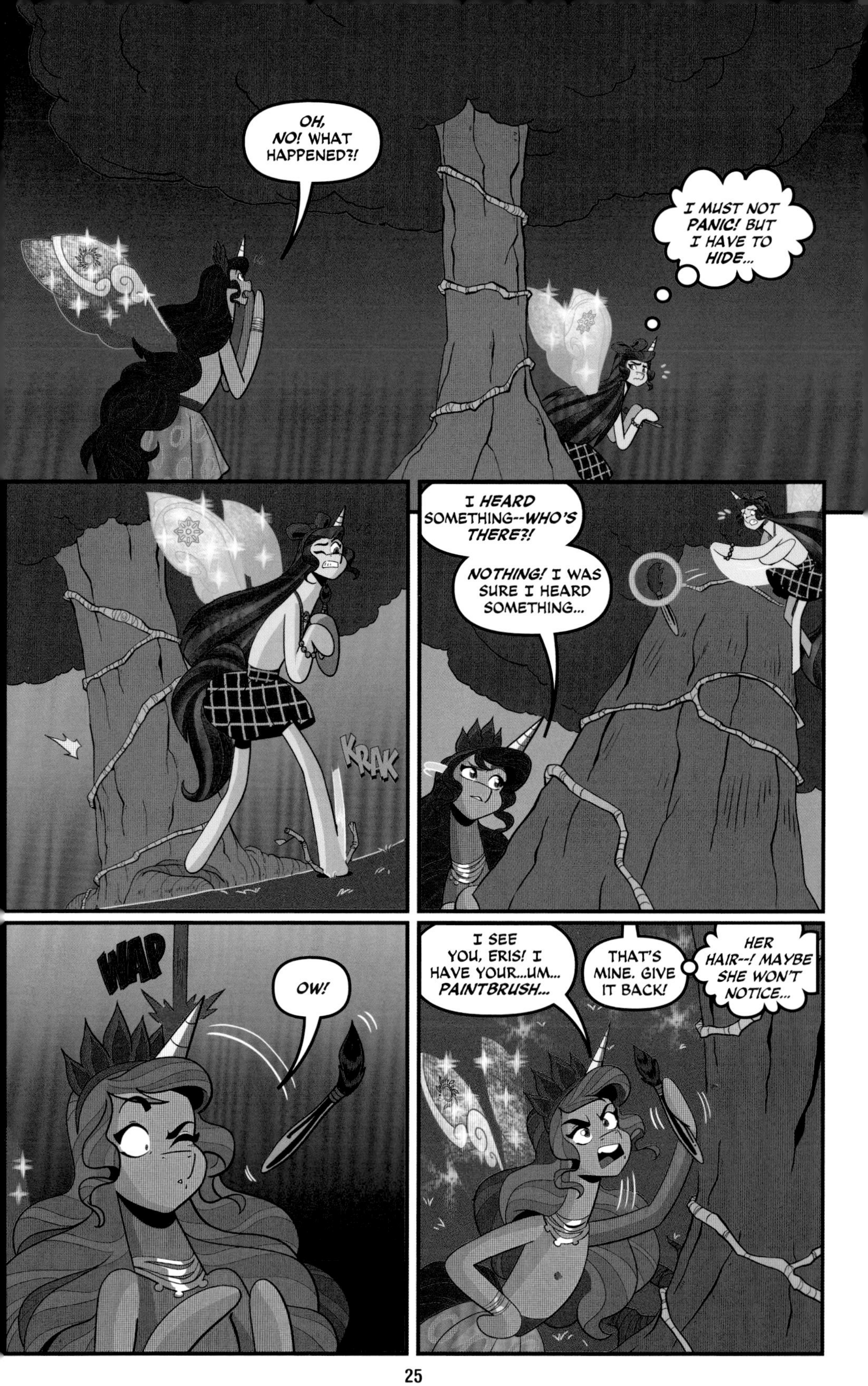

OH, NO! WHAT HAPPENED?!
I MUST NOT PANIC! BUT I HAVE TO HIDE...
KRAK
I HEARD SOMETHING--WHO'S THERE?!
NOTHING! I WAS SURE I HEARD SOMETHING...
WAP
OW!
I SEE YOU, ERIS! I HAVE YOUR...UM... PAINTBRUSH...
THAT'S MINE. GIVE IT BACK!
HER HAIR--! MAYBE SHE WON'T NOTICE...

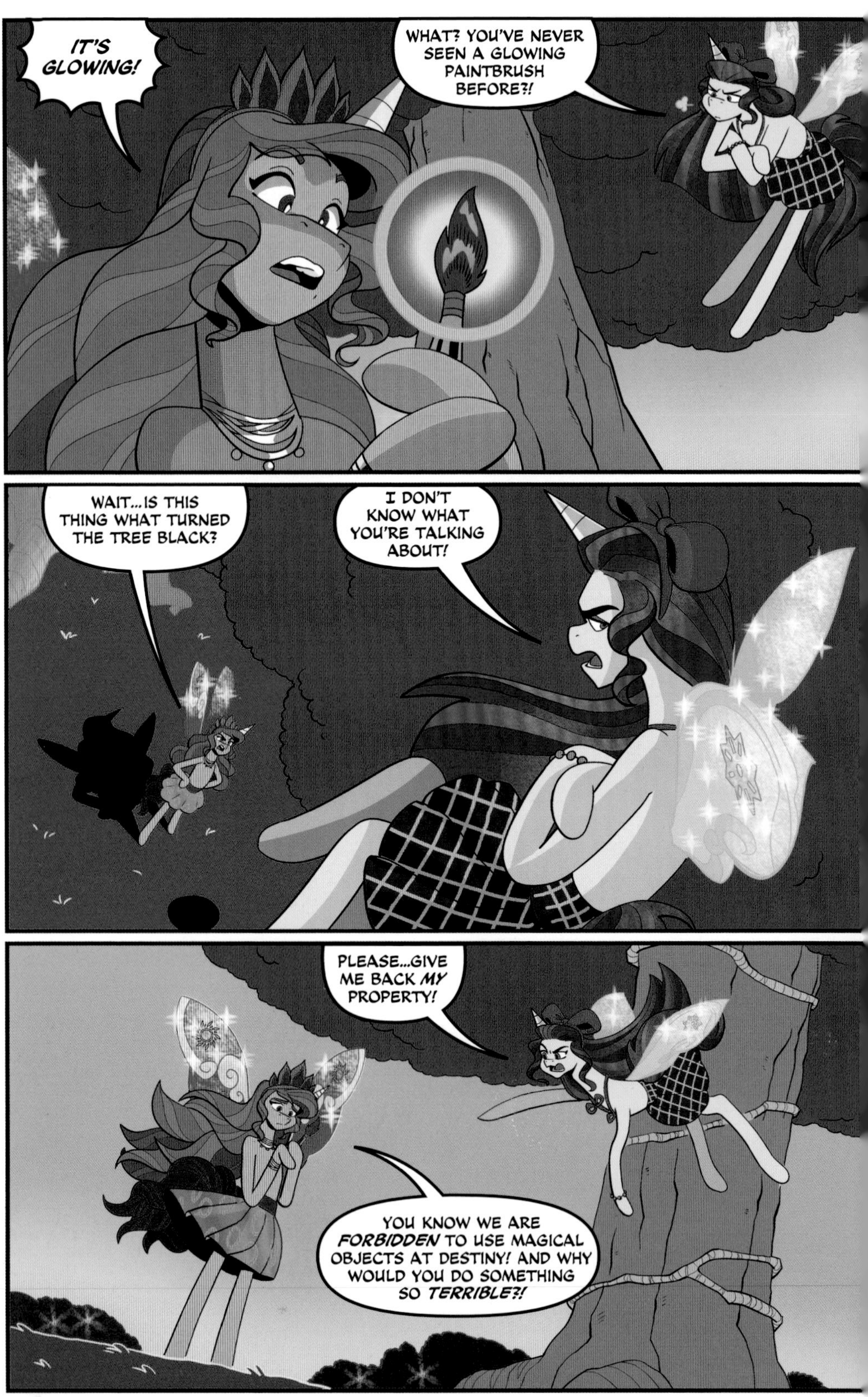
IT'S GLOWING!
WHAT? YOU'VE NEVER SEEN A GLOWING PAINTBRUSH BEFORE?!
WAIT...IS THIS THING WHAT TURNED THE TREE BLACK?
I DON'T KNOW WHAT YOU'RE TALKING ABOUT!
PLEASE...GIVE ME BACK MY PROPERTY!
YOU KNOW WE ARE FORBIDDEN TO USE MAGICAL OBJECTS AT DESTINY! AND WHY WOULD YOU DO SOMETHING SO TERRIBLE?!

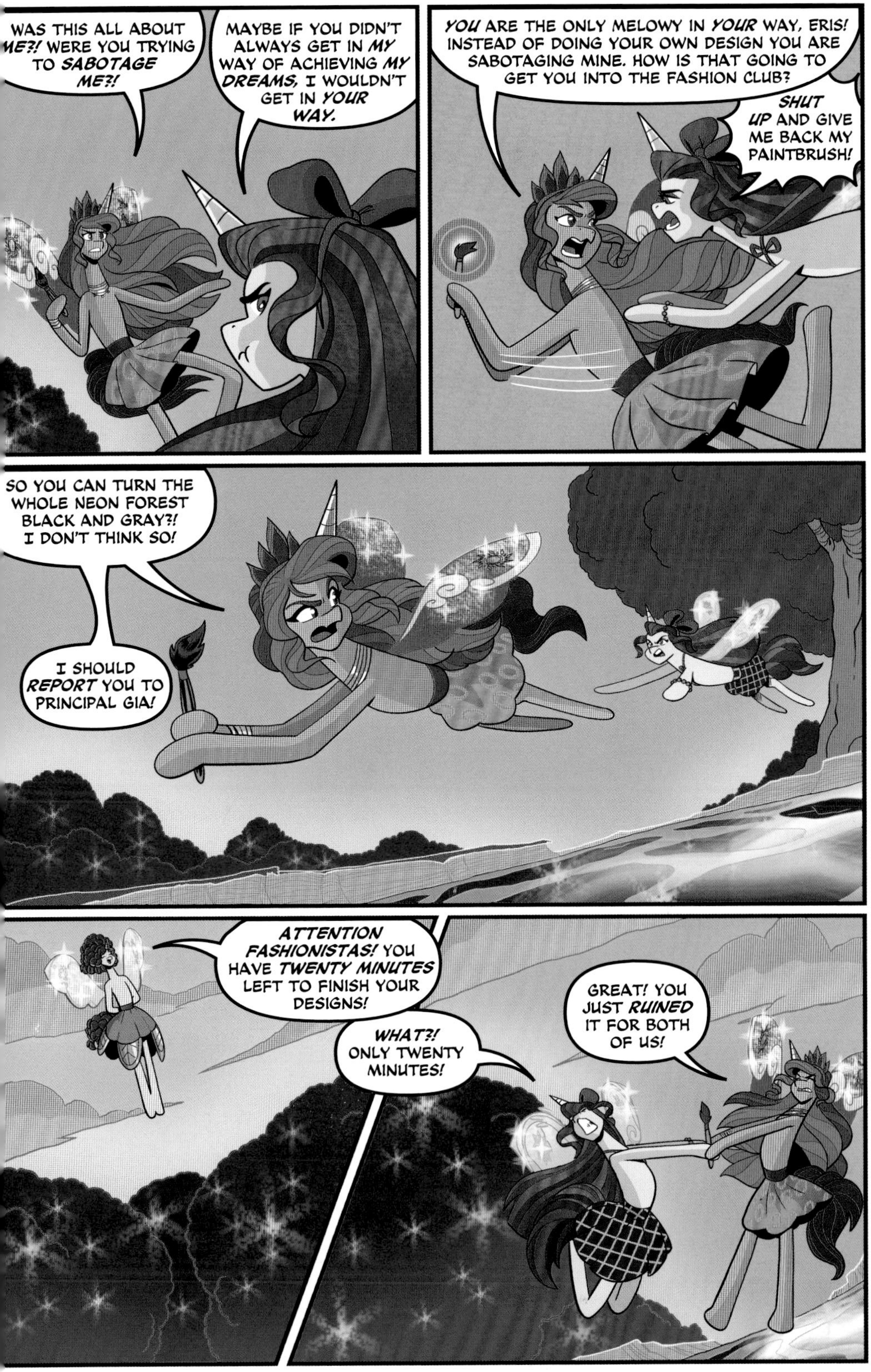
WAS THIS ALL ABOUT ME?! WERE YOU TRYING TO SABOTAGE ME?!
MAYBE IF YOU DIDN'T ALWAYS GET IN MY WAY OF ACHIEVING MY DREAMS, I WOULDN'T GET IN YOUR WAY.
YOU ARE THE ONLY MELOWY IN YOUR WAY, ERIS! INSTEAD OF DOING YOUR OWN DESIGN YOU ARE SABOTAGING MINE. HOW IS THAT GOING TO GET YOU INTO THE FASHION CLUB?
SHUT UP AND GIVE ME BACK MY PAINTBRUSH!
SO YOU CAN TURN THE WHOLE NEON FOREST BLACK AND GRAY?! I DON'T THINK SO!
I SHOULD REPORT YOU TO PRINCIPAL GIA!
ATTENTION FASHIONISTAS! YOU HAVE TWENTY MINUTES LEFT TO FINISH YOUR DESIGNS!
WHAT?! ONLY TWENTY MINUTES!
GREAT! YOU JUST RUINED IT FOR BOTH OF US!

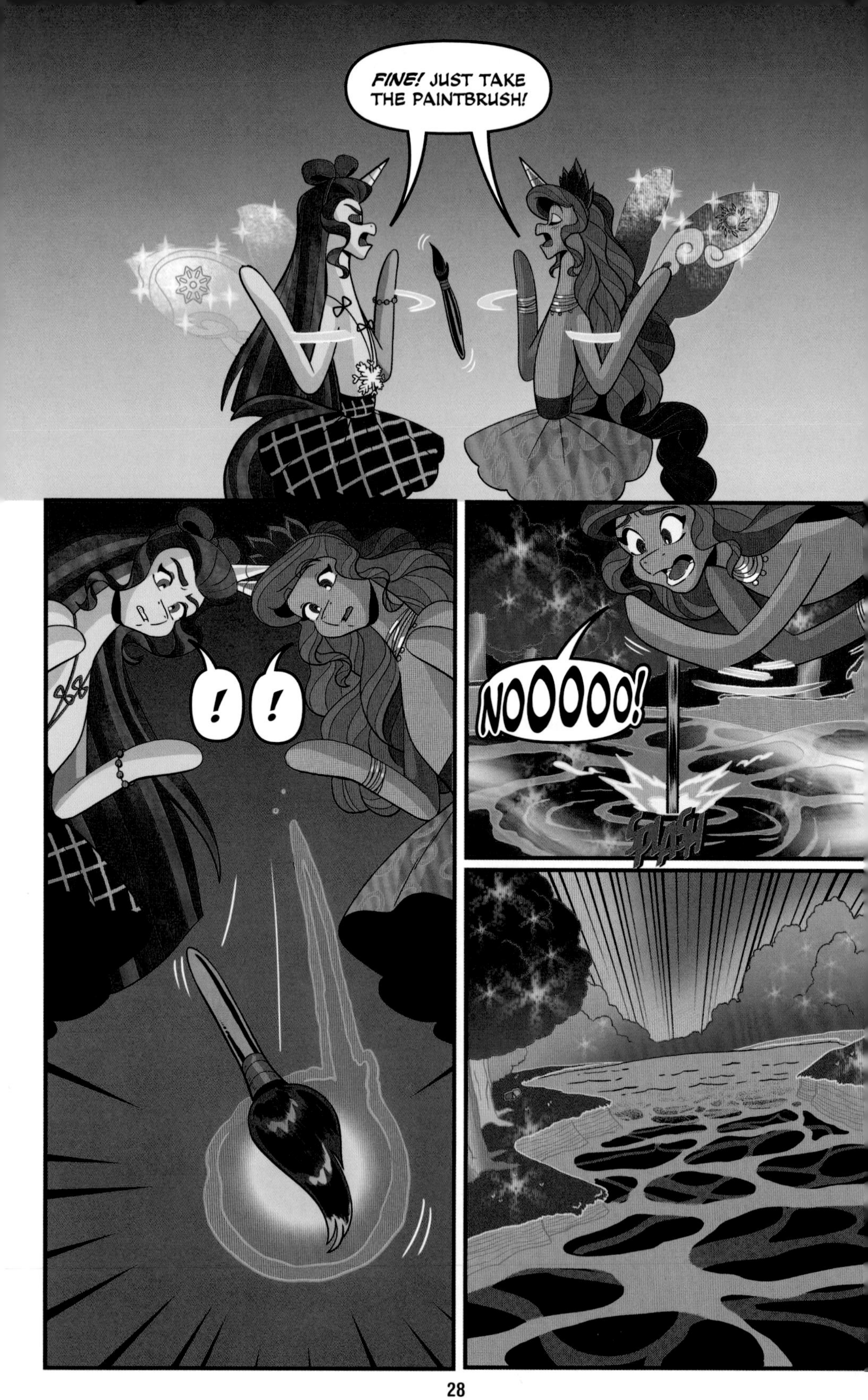
FINE! JUST TAKE THE PAINTBRUSH!
!
!
NOOOOO!
SPLASH

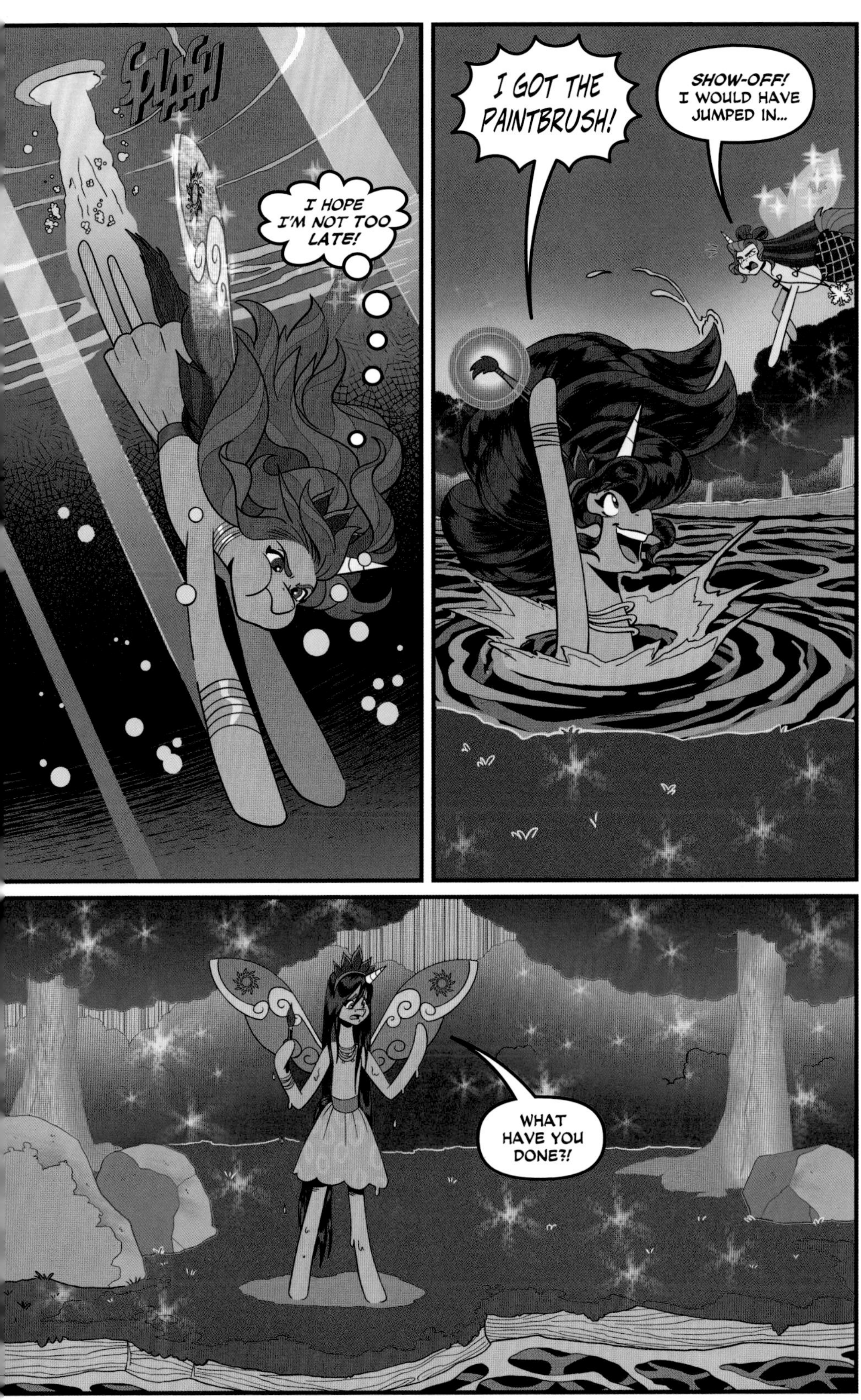
SPLASH
I HOPE I'M NOT TOO LATE!
I GOT THE PAINTBRUSH!
SHOW-OFF! I WOULD HAVE JUMPED IN...
WHAT HAVE YOU DONE?!

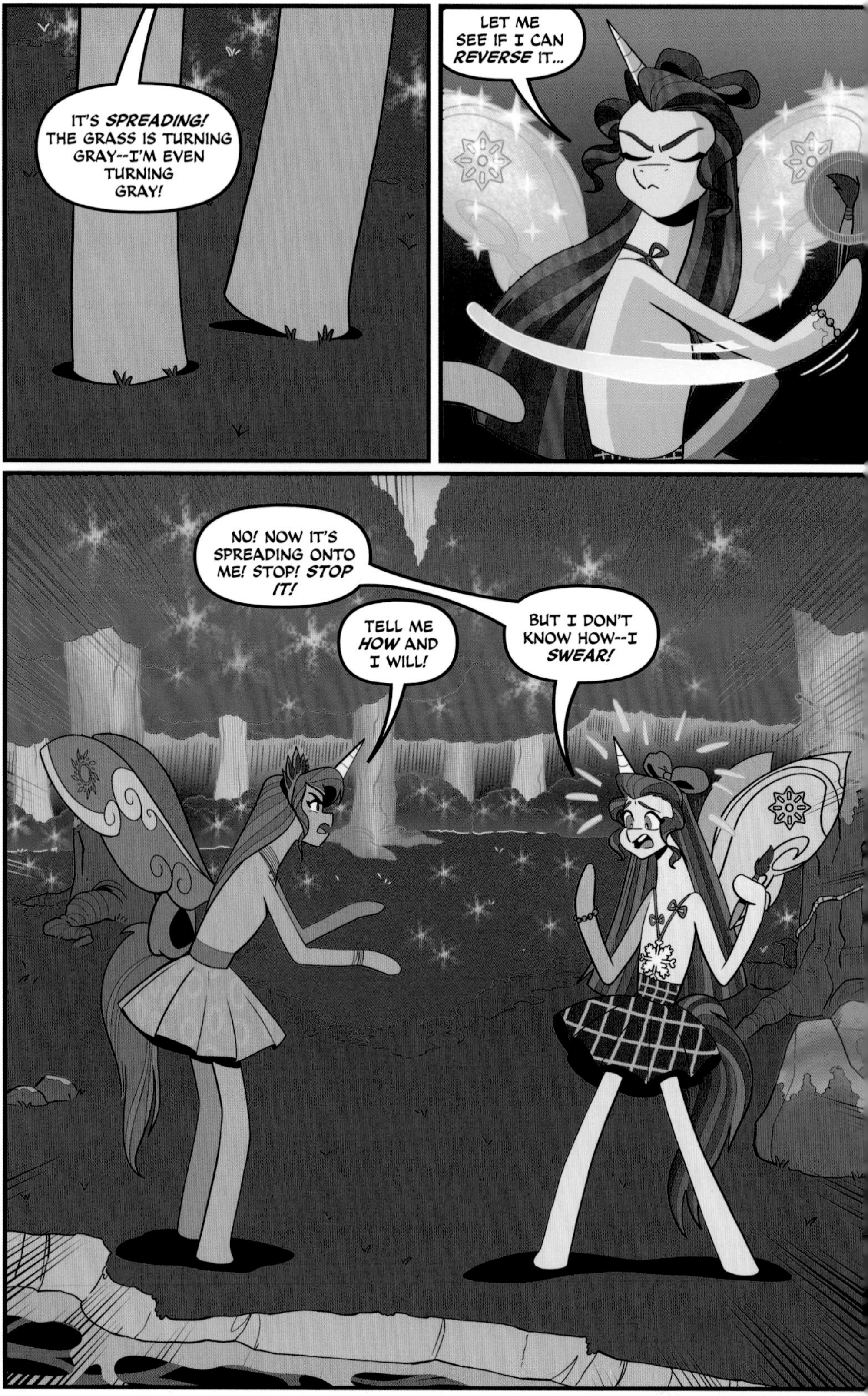
IT'S *SPREADING!* THE GRASS IS TURNING GRAY--I'M EVEN TURNING GRAY!
LET ME SEE IF I CAN *REVERSE* IT...
NO! NOW IT'S SPREADING ONTO ME! STOP! *STOP IT!*
TELL ME *HOW* AND I WILL!
BUT I DON'T KNOW HOW--I *SWEAR!*

UM...THE PETALS ARE GOOD FOR HELPING YOU SLEEP, IF TAKEN AS A TEA...AND CAN WARD OFF BAD DREAMS...THEY GROW ON A PARTICULAR SPOT IN THE SPRING REALM....UM...

CALLED...?

I WONDER HOW ELECTRA AND SELENA ARE DOING. I JUST GOT THIS *WEIRD* FEELING!

YOU HAVE A WEIRD FEELING ABOUT THE FASHION CLUB TRYOUT, CLEO?

IT COULD BE THE BOOK I'M READING, BUT I GOT A *BAD FEELING* IN MY STOMACH... THE SAME ONE I GET WHEN ONE OF US IS IN *TROUBLE*...

I THINK IT'S *YOUR BOOK,* WHAT COULD GO WRONG AT A FASHION TRYOUT?

FOUR REALMS OF PLANTS

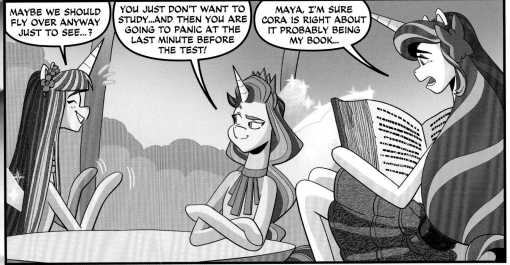

MAYBE WE SHOULD FLY OVER ANYWAY JUST TO SEE...?

YOU JUST DON'T WANT TO STUDY...AND THEN YOU ARE GOING TO PANIC AT THE LAST MINUTE BEFORE THE TEST!

MAYA, I'M SURE CORA IS RIGHT ABOUT IT PROBABLY BEING MY BOOK...

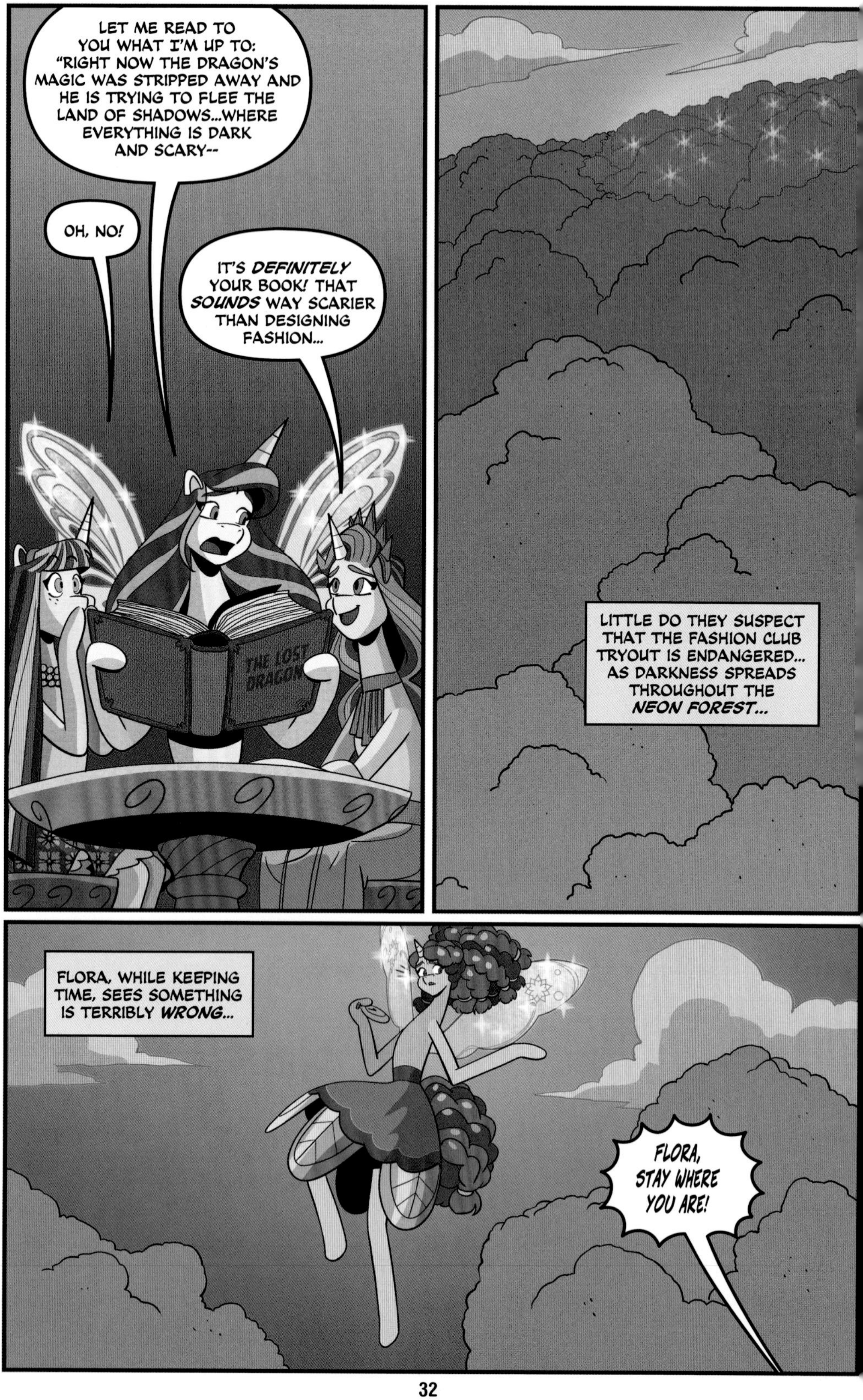
LET ME READ TO YOU WHAT I'M UP TO: "RIGHT NOW THE DRAGON'S MAGIC WAS STRIPPED AWAY AND HE IS TRYING TO FLEE THE LAND OF SHADOWS...WHERE EVERYTHING IS DARK AND SCARY--
OH, NO!
IT'S *DEFINITELY* YOUR BOOK! THAT *SOUNDS* WAY SCARIER THAN DESIGNING FASHION...
THE LOST DRAGON
LITTLE DO THEY SUSPECT THAT THE FASHION CLUB TRYOUT IS ENDANGERED... AS DARKNESS SPREADS THROUGHOUT THE *NEON FOREST*...
FLORA, WHILE KEEPING TIME, SEES SOMETHING IS TERRIBLY *WRONG*...
FLORA, STAY WHERE YOU ARE!

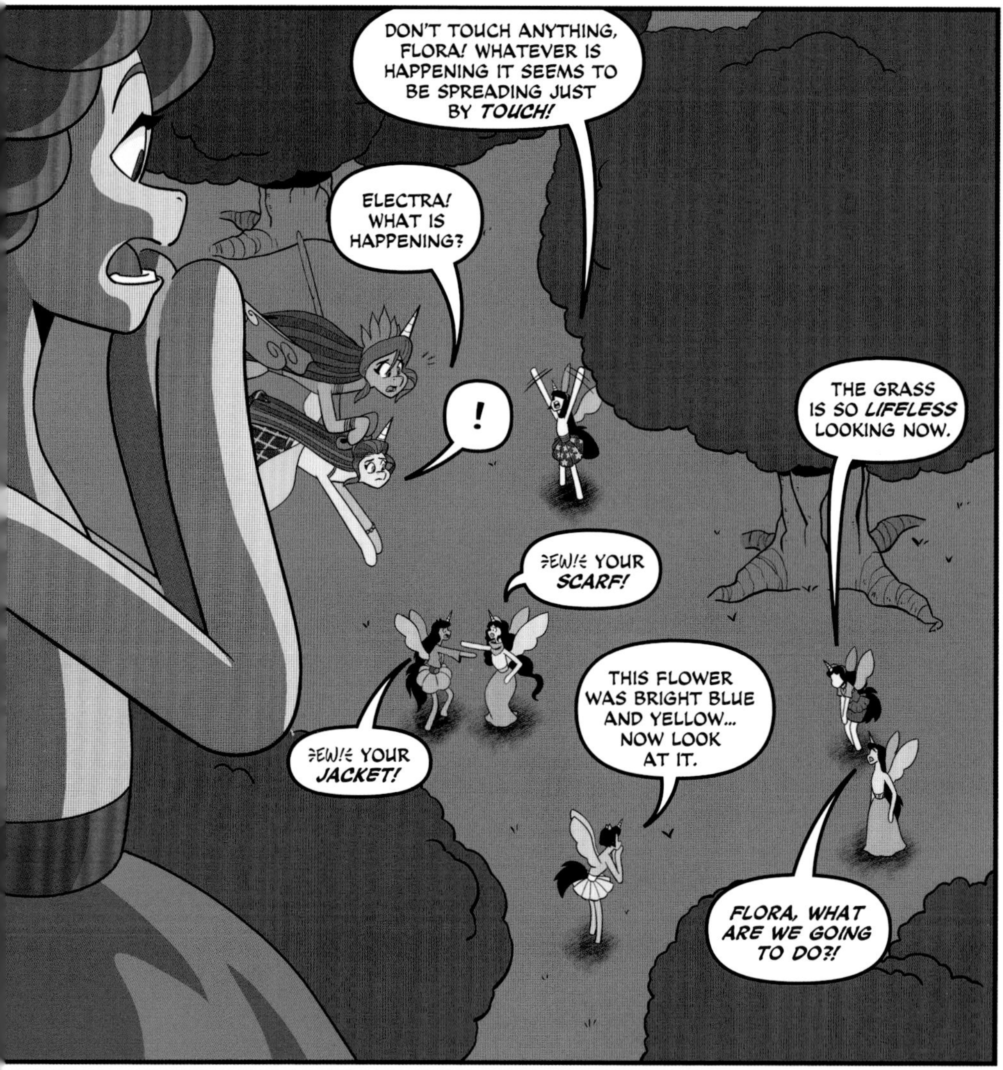
DON'T TOUCH ANYTHING, FLORA! WHATEVER IS HAPPENING IT SEEMS TO BE SPREADING JUST BY *TOUCH!*
ELECTRA! WHAT IS HAPPENING?
!
THE GRASS IS SO *LIFELESS* LOOKING NOW.
EW! YOUR *SCARF!*
EW! YOUR *JACKET!*
THIS FLOWER WAS BRIGHT BLUE AND YELLOW... NOW LOOK AT IT.
FLORA, WHAT ARE WE GOING TO DO?!

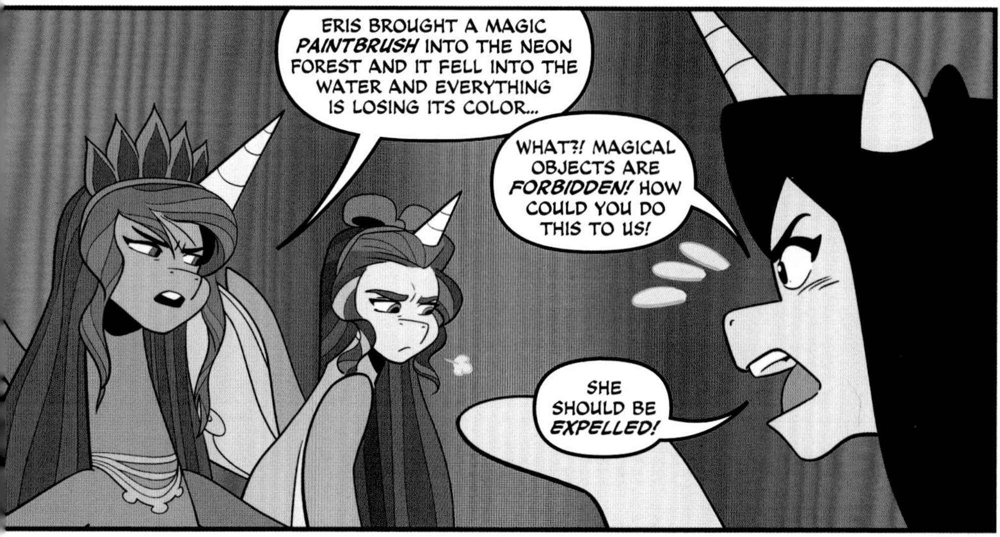
ERIS BROUGHT A MAGIC *PAINTBRUSH* INTO THE NEON FOREST AND IT FELL INTO THE WATER AND EVERYTHING IS LOSING ITS COLOR...
WHAT?! MAGICAL OBJECTS ARE *FORBIDDEN!* HOW COULD YOU DO THIS TO US!
SHE SHOULD BE *EXPELLED!*

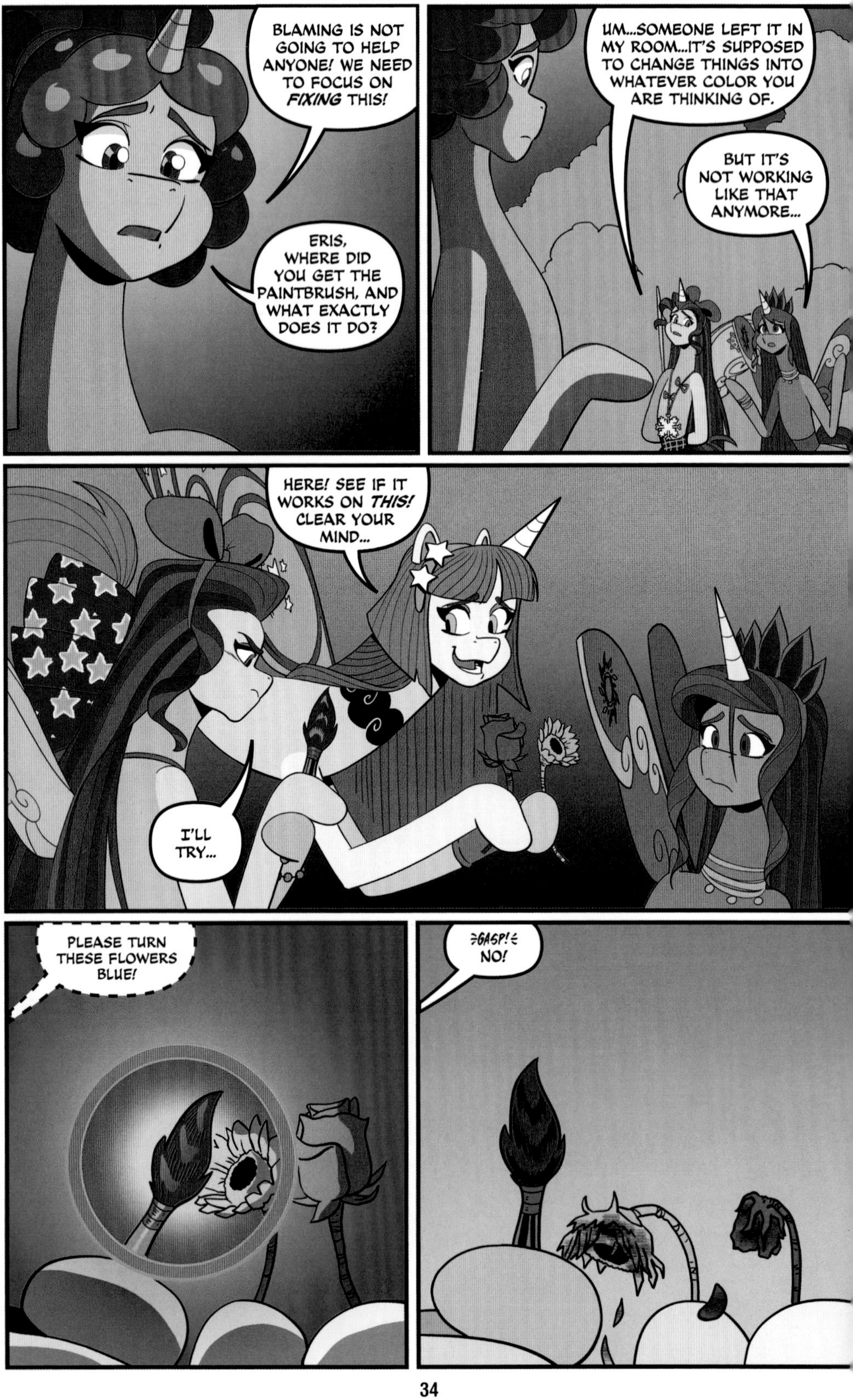
BLAMING IS NOT GOING TO HELP ANYONE! WE NEED TO FOCUS ON *FIXING* THIS!
ERIS, WHERE DID YOU GET THE PAINTBRUSH, AND WHAT EXACTLY DOES IT DO?
UM...SOMEONE LEFT IT IN MY ROOM...IT'S SUPPOSED TO CHANGE THINGS INTO WHATEVER COLOR YOU ARE THINKING OF.
BUT IT'S NOT WORKING LIKE THAT ANYMORE...
HERE! SEE IF IT WORKS ON *THIS!* CLEAR YOUR MIND...
I'LL TRY...
PLEASE TURN THESE FLOWERS BLUE!
GASP!
NO!

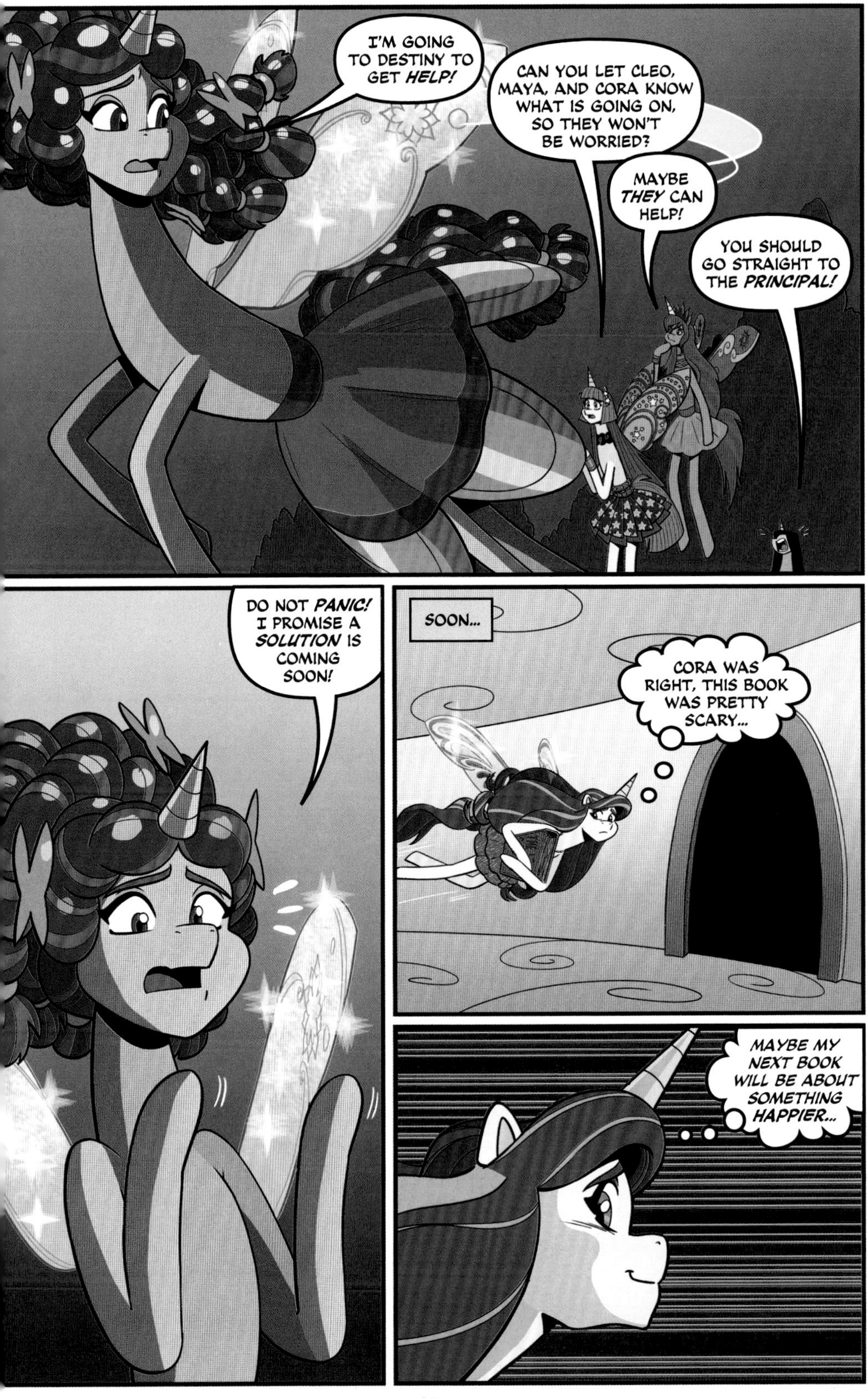
I'M GOING TO DESTINY TO GET HELP!
CAN YOU LET CLEO, MAYA, AND CORA KNOW WHAT IS GOING ON, SO THEY WON'T BE WORRIED?
MAYBE THEY CAN HELP!
YOU SHOULD GO STRAIGHT TO THE PRINCIPAL!
DO NOT PANIC! I PROMISE A SOLUTION IS COMING SOON!
SOON...
CORA WAS RIGHT, THIS BOOK WAS PRETTY SCARY...
MAYBE MY NEXT BOOK WILL BE ABOUT SOMETHING HAPPIER...

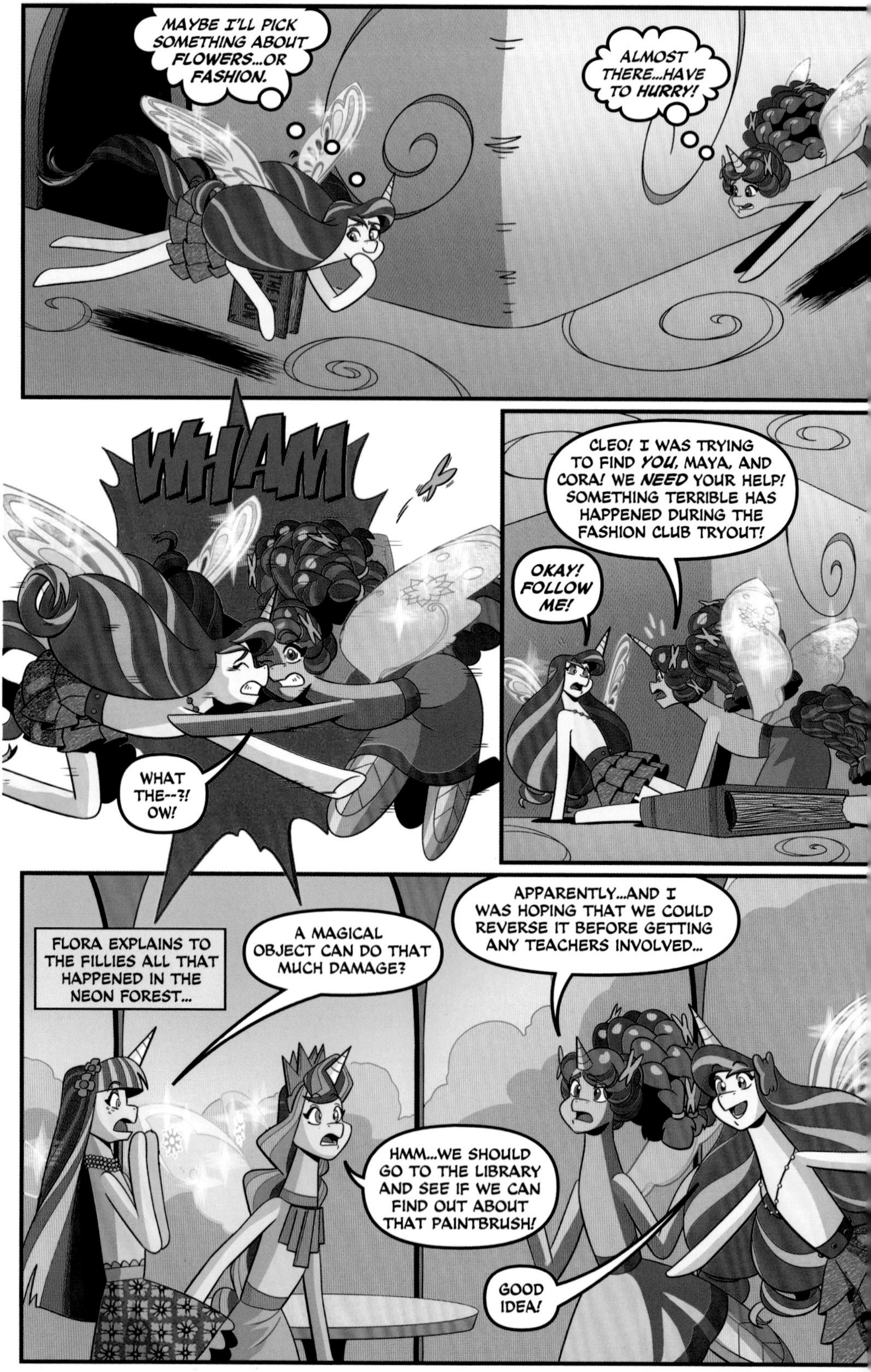
MAYBE I'LL PICK SOMETHING ABOUT FLOWERS...OR FASHION.
ALMOST THERE...HAVE TO HURRY!
WHAM
WHAT THE--?! OW!
CLEO! I WAS TRYING TO FIND YOU, MAYA, AND CORA! WE NEED YOUR HELP! SOMETHING TERRIBLE HAS HAPPENED DURING THE FASHION CLUB TRYOUT!
OKAY! FOLLOW ME!
FLORA EXPLAINS TO THE FILLIES ALL THAT HAPPENED IN THE NEON FOREST...
A MAGICAL OBJECT CAN DO THAT MUCH DAMAGE?
APPARENTLY...AND I WAS HOPING THAT WE COULD REVERSE IT BEFORE GETTING ANY TEACHERS INVOLVED...
HMM...WE SHOULD GO TO THE LIBRARY AND SEE IF WE CAN FIND OUT ABOUT THAT PAINTBRUSH!
GOOD IDEA!

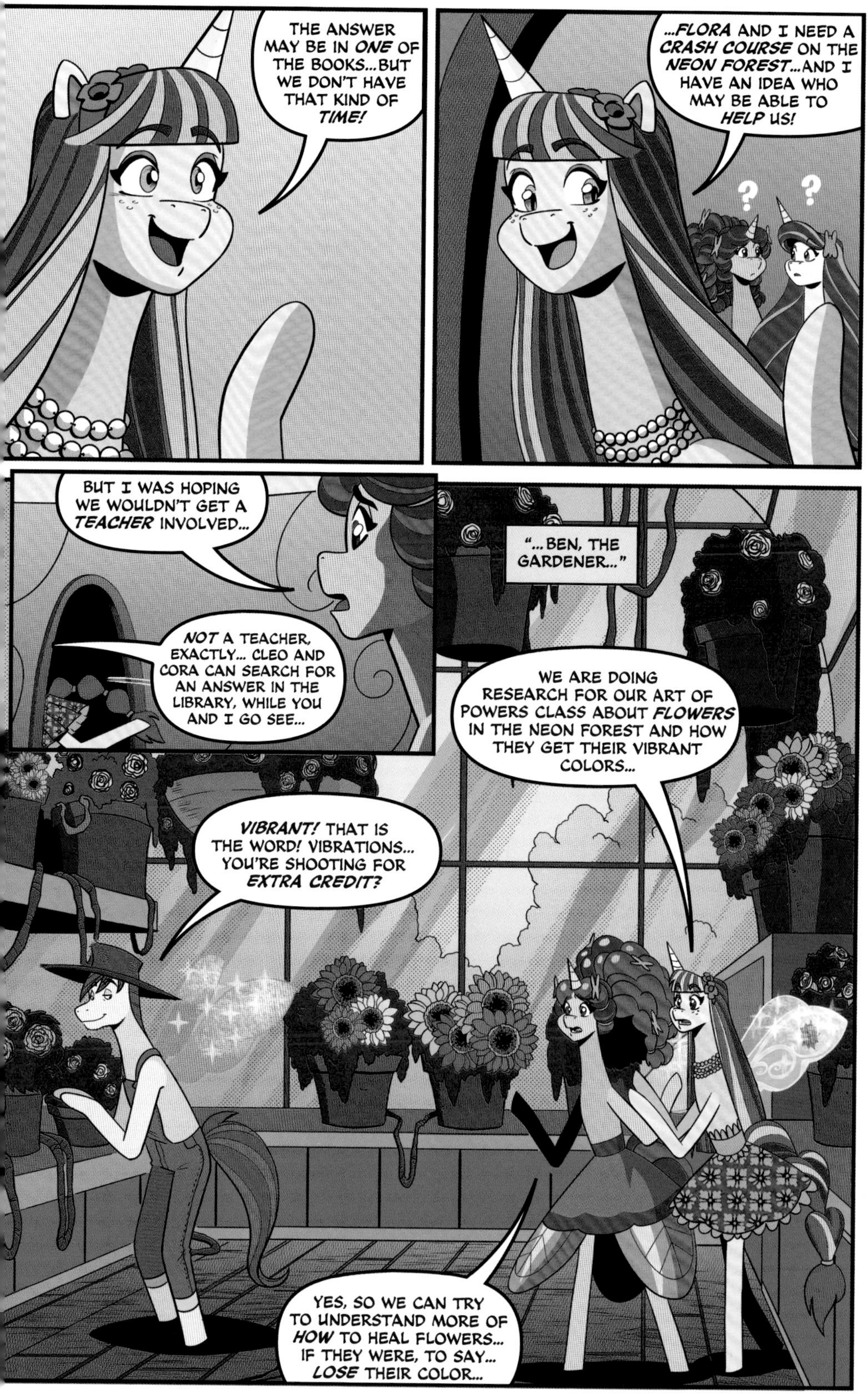
THE ANSWER MAY BE IN *ONE* OF THE BOOKS...BUT WE DON'T HAVE THAT KIND OF *TIME!*
...*FLORA* AND I NEED A *CRASH COURSE* ON THE *NEON FOREST*...AND I HAVE AN IDEA WHO MAY BE ABLE TO *HELP* US!
?
?
BUT I WAS HOPING WE WOULDN'T GET A *TEACHER* INVOLVED...
NOT A TEACHER, EXACTLY... CLEO AND CORA CAN SEARCH FOR AN ANSWER IN THE LIBRARY, WHILE YOU AND I GO SEE...
"...BEN, THE GARDENER..."
WE ARE DOING RESEARCH FOR OUR ART OF POWERS CLASS ABOUT *FLOWERS* IN THE NEON FOREST AND HOW THEY GET THEIR VIBRANT COLORS...
VIBRANT! THAT IS THE WORD! VIBRATIONS... YOU'RE SHOOTING FOR *EXTRA CREDIT?*
YES, SO WE CAN TRY TO UNDERSTAND MORE OF *HOW* TO HEAL FLOWERS... IF THEY WERE, TO SAY... *LOSE* THEIR COLOR...

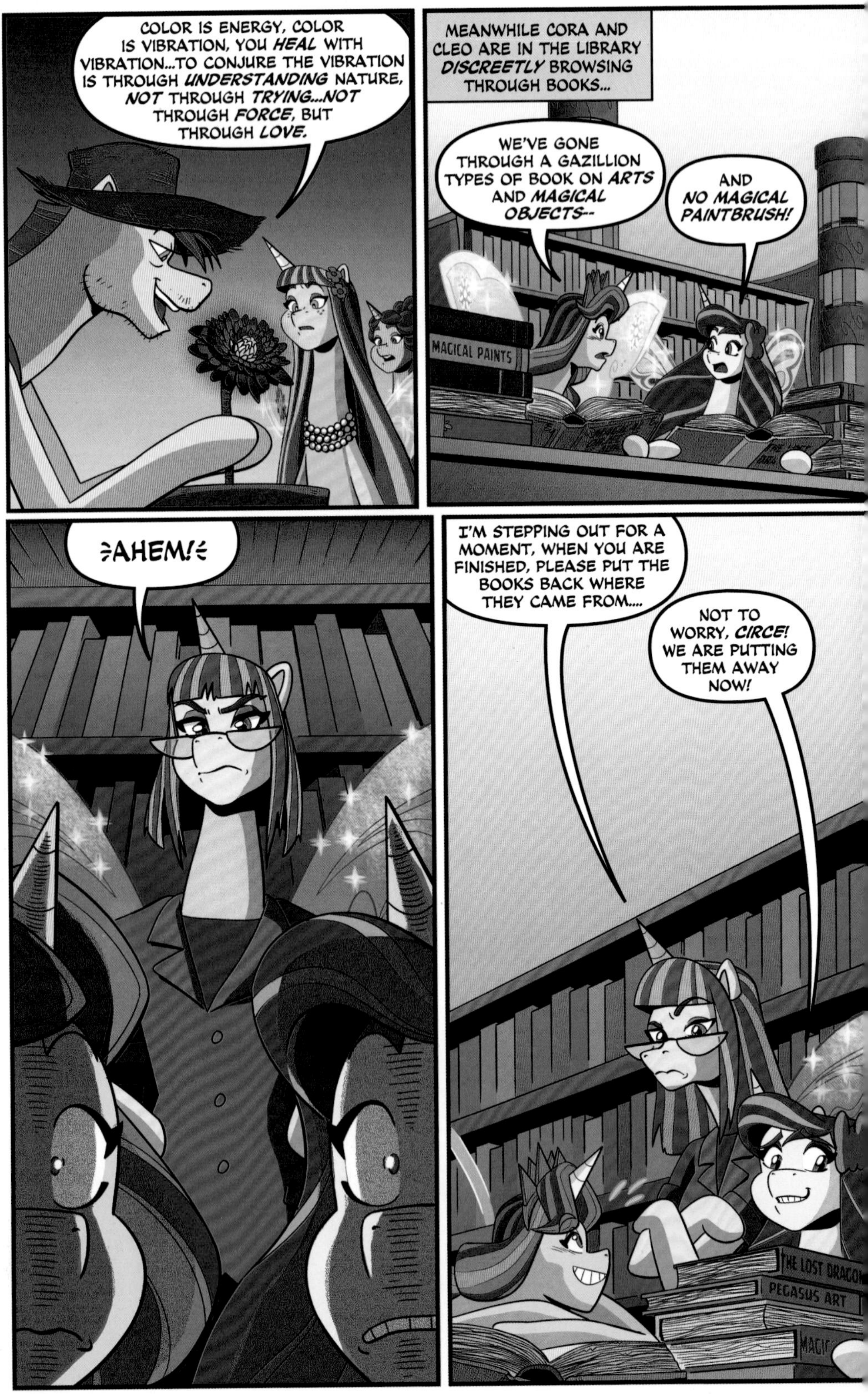
COLOR IS ENERGY, COLOR IS VIBRATION, YOU HEAL WITH VIBRATION...TO CONJURE THE VIBRATION IS THROUGH UNDERSTANDING NATURE, NOT THROUGH TRYING...NOT THROUGH FORCE, BUT THROUGH LOVE.
MEANWHILE CORA AND CLEO ARE IN THE LIBRARY DISCREETLY BROWSING THROUGH BOOKS...
WE'VE GONE THROUGH A GAZILLION TYPES OF BOOK ON ARTS AND MAGICAL OBJECTS--
AND NO MAGICAL PAINTBRUSH!
MAGICAL PAINTS
AHEM!
I'M STEPPING OUT FOR A MOMENT, WHEN YOU ARE FINISHED, PLEASE PUT THE BOOKS BACK WHERE THEY CAME FROM....
NOT TO WORRY, CIRCE! WE ARE PUTTING THEM AWAY NOW!
THE LOST DRAGON
PEGASUS ART
MAGIC

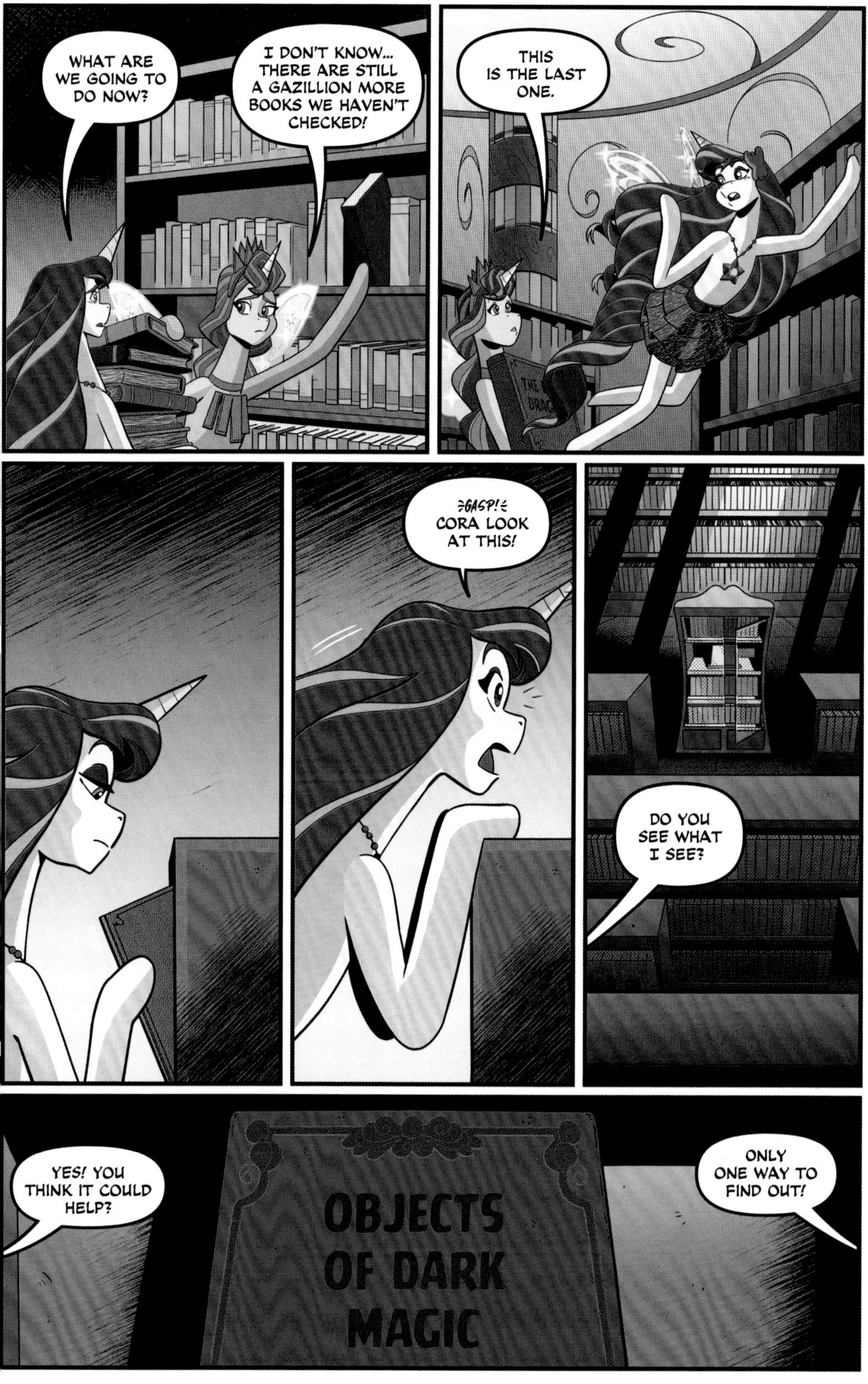

WHAT ARE WE GOING TO DO NOW?
I DON'T KNOW... THERE ARE STILL A GAZILLION MORE BOOKS WE HAVEN'T CHECKED!
THIS IS THE LAST ONE.
GASP! CORA LOOK AT THIS!
DO YOU SEE WHAT I SEE?
YES! YOU THINK IT COULD HELP?
OBJECTS OF DARK MAGIC
ONLY ONE WAY TO FIND OUT!

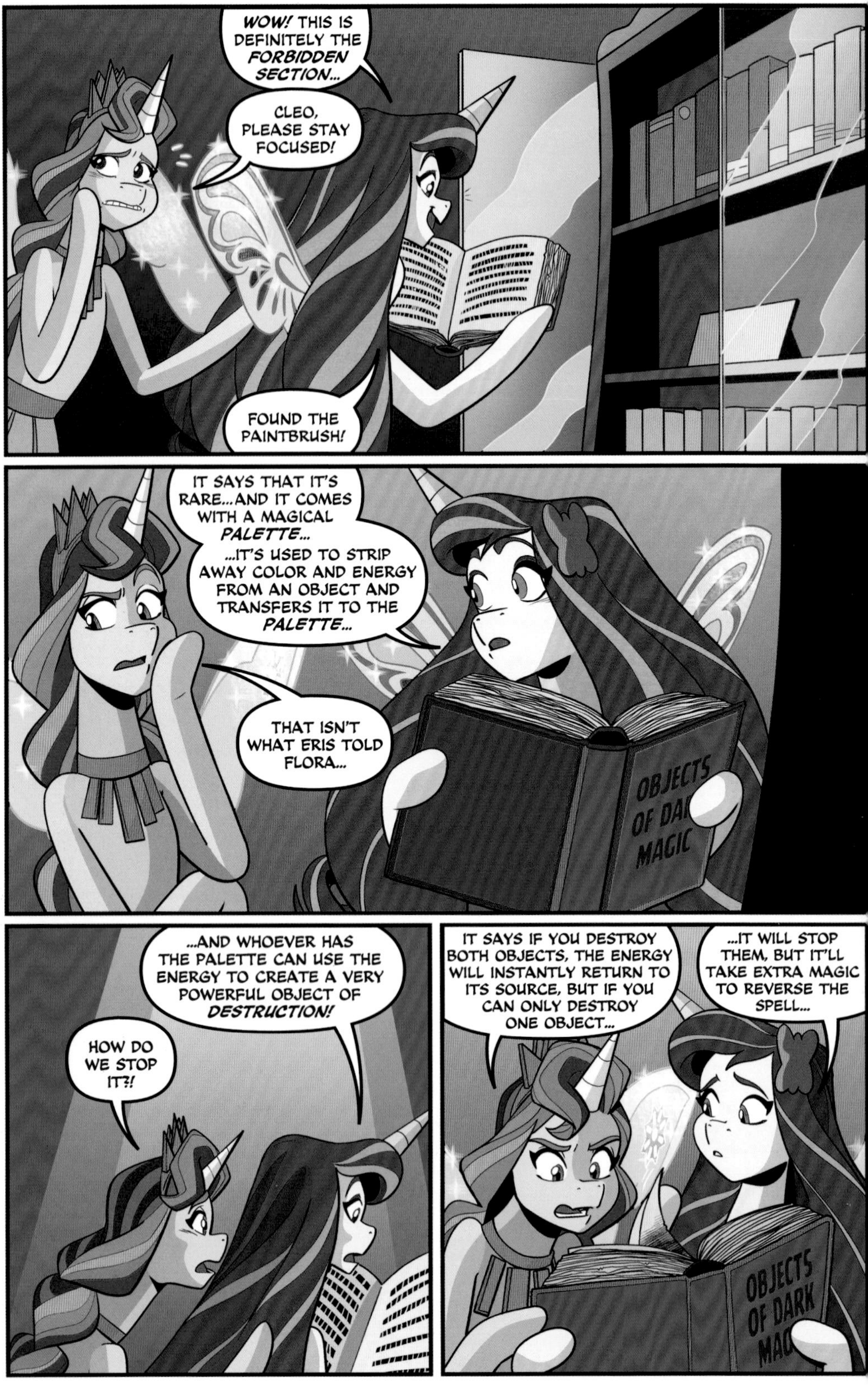
WOW! THIS IS DEFINITELY THE FORBIDDEN SECTION...
CLEO, PLEASE STAY FOCUSED!
FOUND THE PAINTBRUSH!
IT SAYS THAT IT'S RARE...AND IT COMES WITH A MAGICAL PALETTE...
...IT'S USED TO STRIP AWAY COLOR AND ENERGY FROM AN OBJECT AND TRANSFERS IT TO THE PALETTE...
THAT ISN'T WHAT ERIS TOLD FLORA...
OBJECTS OF DARK MAGIC
...AND WHOEVER HAS THE PALETTE CAN USE THE ENERGY TO CREATE A VERY POWERFUL OBJECT OF DESTRUCTION!
HOW DO WE STOP IT?!
IT SAYS IF YOU DESTROY BOTH OBJECTS, THE ENERGY WILL INSTANTLY RETURN TO ITS SOURCE, BUT IF YOU CAN ONLY DESTROY ONE OBJECT...
...IT WILL STOP THEM, BUT IT'LL TAKE EXTRA MAGIC TO REVERSE THE SPELL...
OBJECTS OF DARK

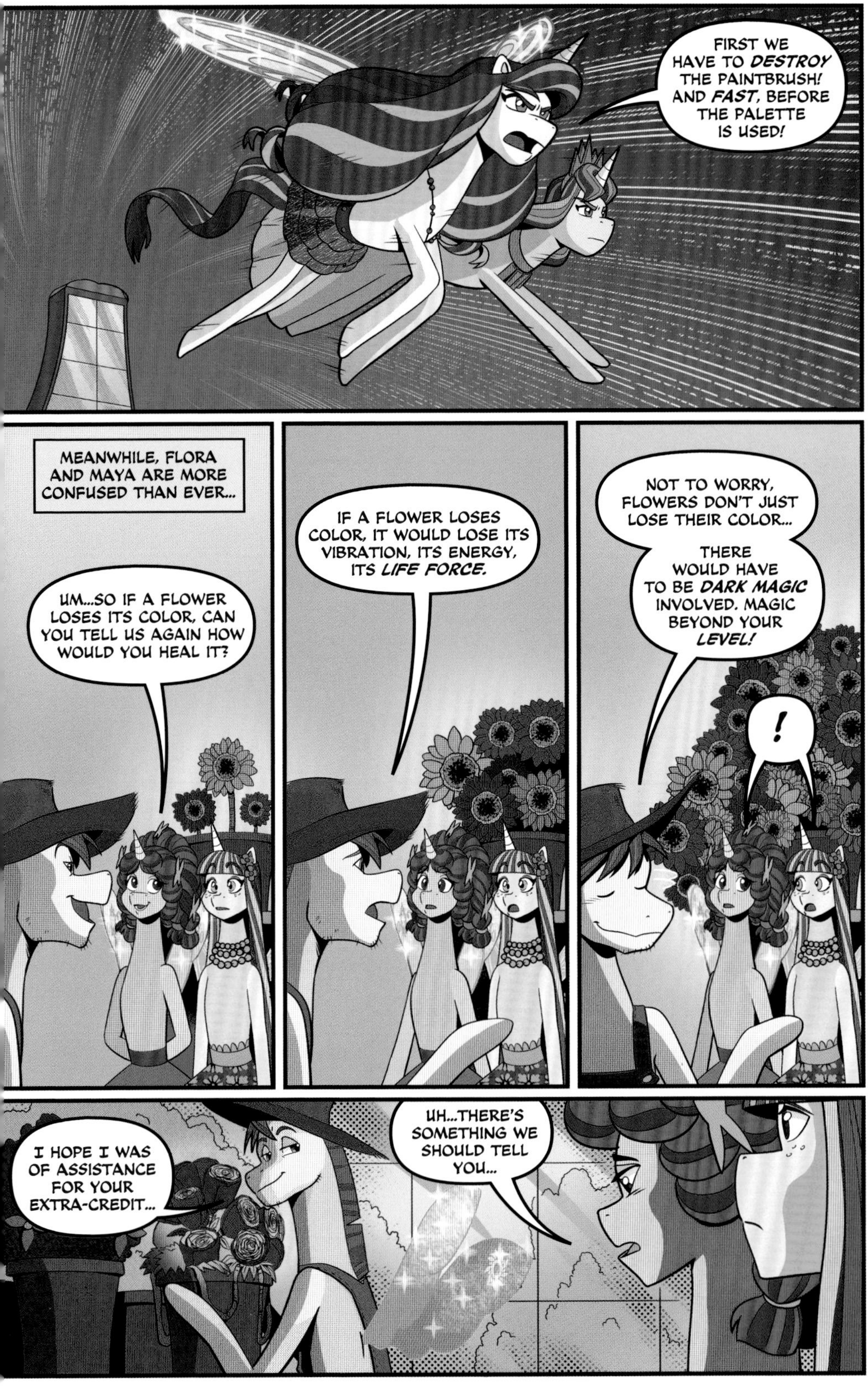
FIRST WE HAVE TO *DESTROY* THE PAINTBRUSH! AND *FAST*, BEFORE THE PALETTE IS USED!
MEANWHILE, FLORA AND MAYA ARE MORE CONFUSED THAN EVER...
UM...SO IF A FLOWER LOSES ITS COLOR, CAN YOU TELL US AGAIN HOW WOULD YOU HEAL IT?
IF A FLOWER LOSES COLOR, IT WOULD LOSE ITS VIBRATION, ITS ENERGY, ITS *LIFE FORCE.*
NOT TO WORRY, FLOWERS DON'T JUST LOSE THEIR COLOR...
THERE WOULD HAVE TO BE *DARK MAGIC* INVOLVED. MAGIC BEYOND YOUR *LEVEL!*
!
I HOPE I WAS OF ASSISTANCE FOR YOUR EXTRA-CREDIT...
UH...THERE'S SOMETHING WE SHOULD TELL YOU...

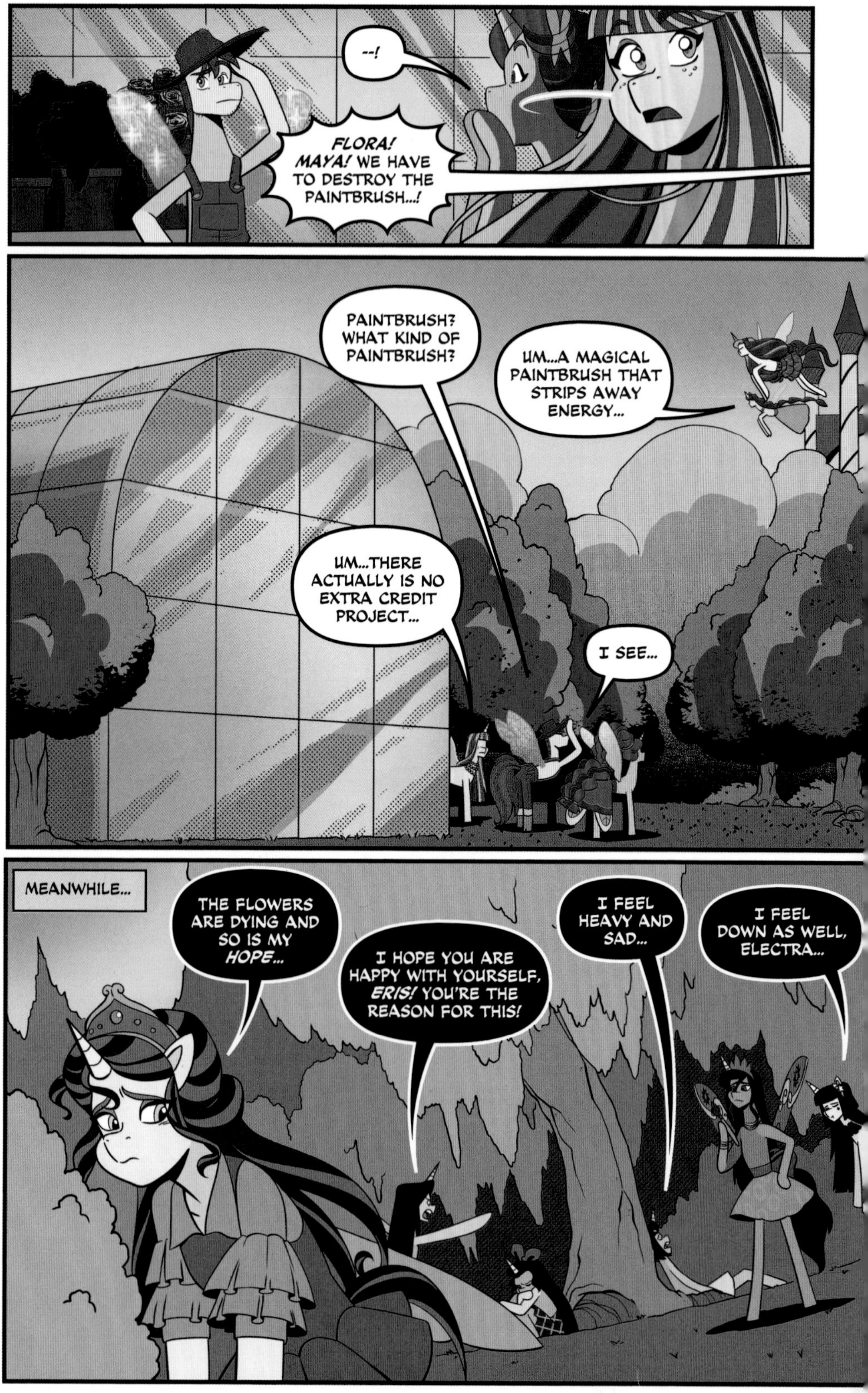
--!
FLORA! MAYA! WE HAVE TO DESTROY THE PAINTBRUSH...!
PAINTBRUSH? WHAT KIND OF PAINTBRUSH?
UM...A MAGICAL PAINTBRUSH THAT STRIPS AWAY ENERGY...
UM...THERE ACTUALLY IS NO EXTRA CREDIT PROJECT...
I SEE...
MEANWHILE...
THE FLOWERS ARE DYING AND SO IS MY HOPE...
I HOPE YOU ARE HAPPY WITH YOURSELF, ERIS! YOU'RE THE REASON FOR THIS!
I FEEL HEAVY AND SAD...
I FEEL DOWN AS WELL, ELECTRA...

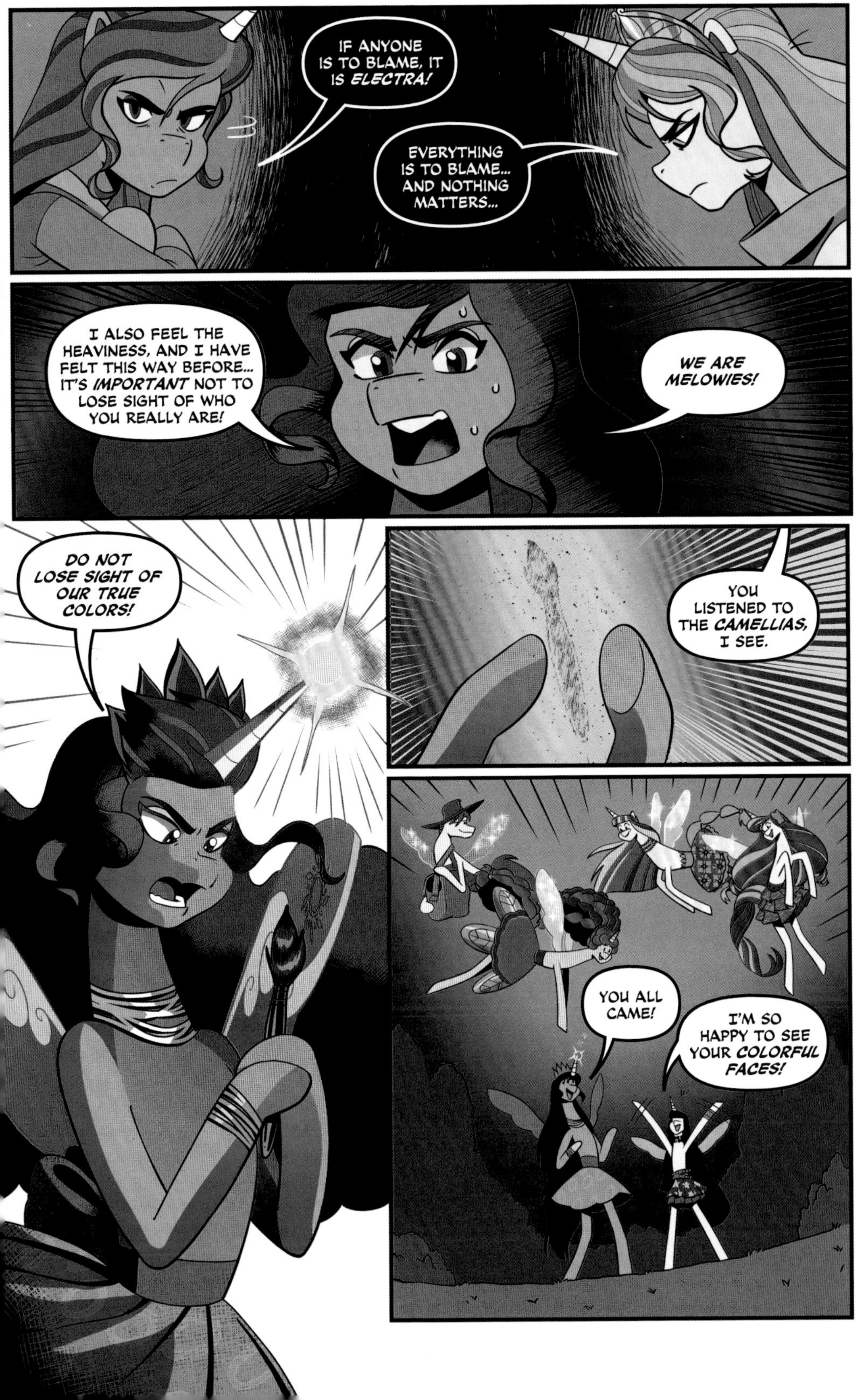
IF ANYONE IS TO BLAME, IT IS *ELECTRA!*
EVERYTHING IS TO BLAME... AND NOTHING MATTERS...
I ALSO FEEL THE HEAVINESS, AND I HAVE FELT THIS WAY BEFORE... IT'S *IMPORTANT* NOT TO LOSE SIGHT OF WHO YOU REALLY ARE!
WE ARE MELOWIES!
DO NOT LOSE SIGHT OF OUR TRUE COLORS!
YOU LISTENED TO THE *CAMELLIAS,* I SEE.
YOU ALL CAME!
I'M SO HAPPY TO SEE YOUR *COLORFUL FACES!*

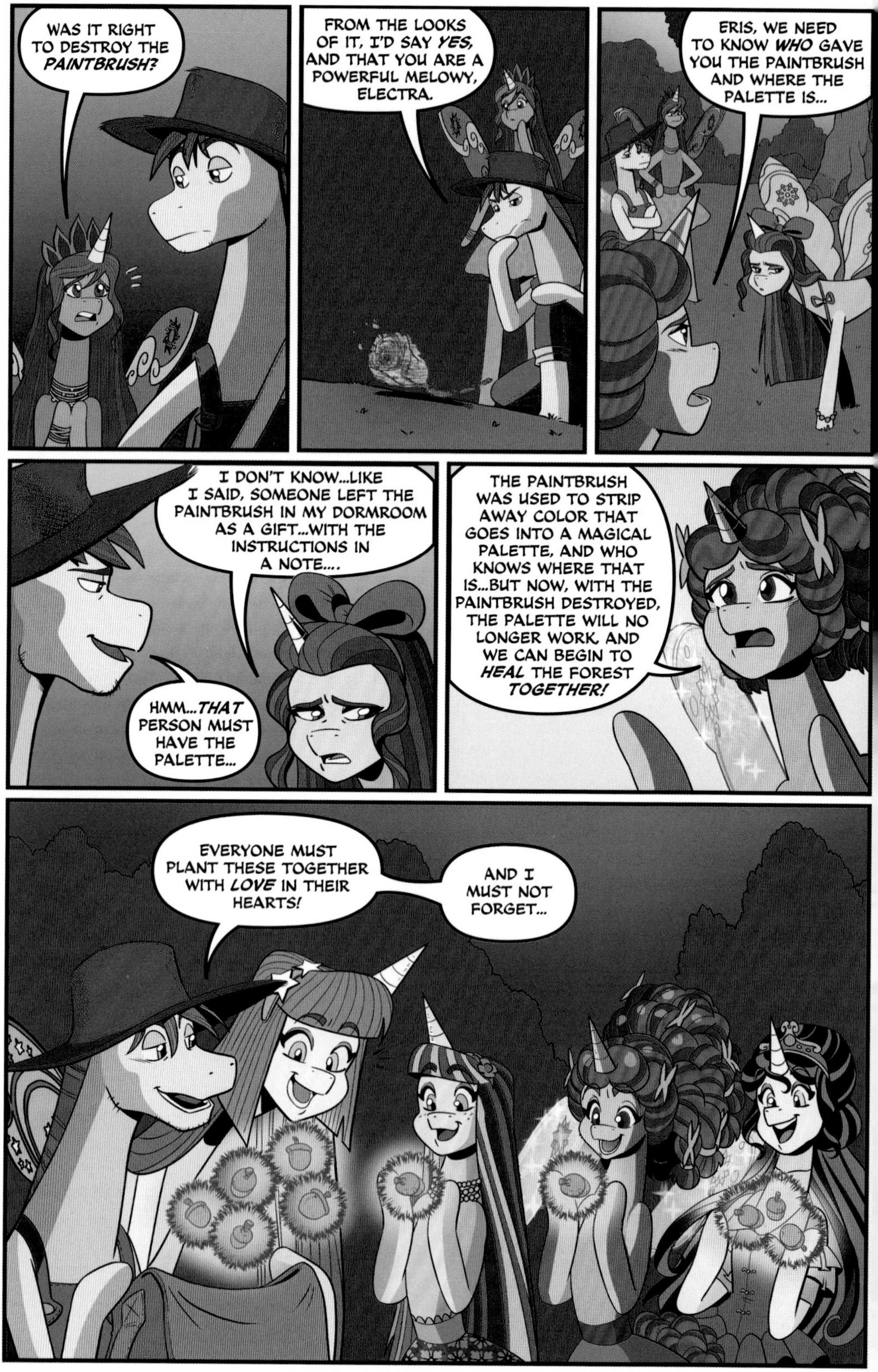
WAS IT RIGHT TO DESTROY THE *PAINTBRUSH?*
FROM THE LOOKS OF IT, I'D SAY *YES,* AND THAT YOU ARE A POWERFUL MELOWY, ELECTRA.
ERIS, WE NEED TO KNOW *WHO* GAVE YOU THE PAINTBRUSH AND WHERE THE PALETTE IS...
I DON'T KNOW...LIKE I SAID, SOMEONE LEFT THE PAINTBRUSH IN MY DORMROOM AS A GIFT...WITH THE INSTRUCTIONS IN A NOTE....
HMM...*THAT* PERSON MUST HAVE THE PALETTE...
THE PAINTBRUSH WAS USED TO STRIP AWAY COLOR THAT GOES INTO A MAGICAL PALETTE, AND WHO KNOWS WHERE THAT IS...BUT NOW, WITH THE PAINTBRUSH DESTROYED, THE PALETTE WILL NO LONGER WORK, AND WE CAN BEGIN TO *HEAL* THE FOREST *TOGETHER!*
EVERYONE MUST PLANT THESE TOGETHER WITH *LOVE* IN THEIR HEARTS!
AND I MUST NOT FORGET...

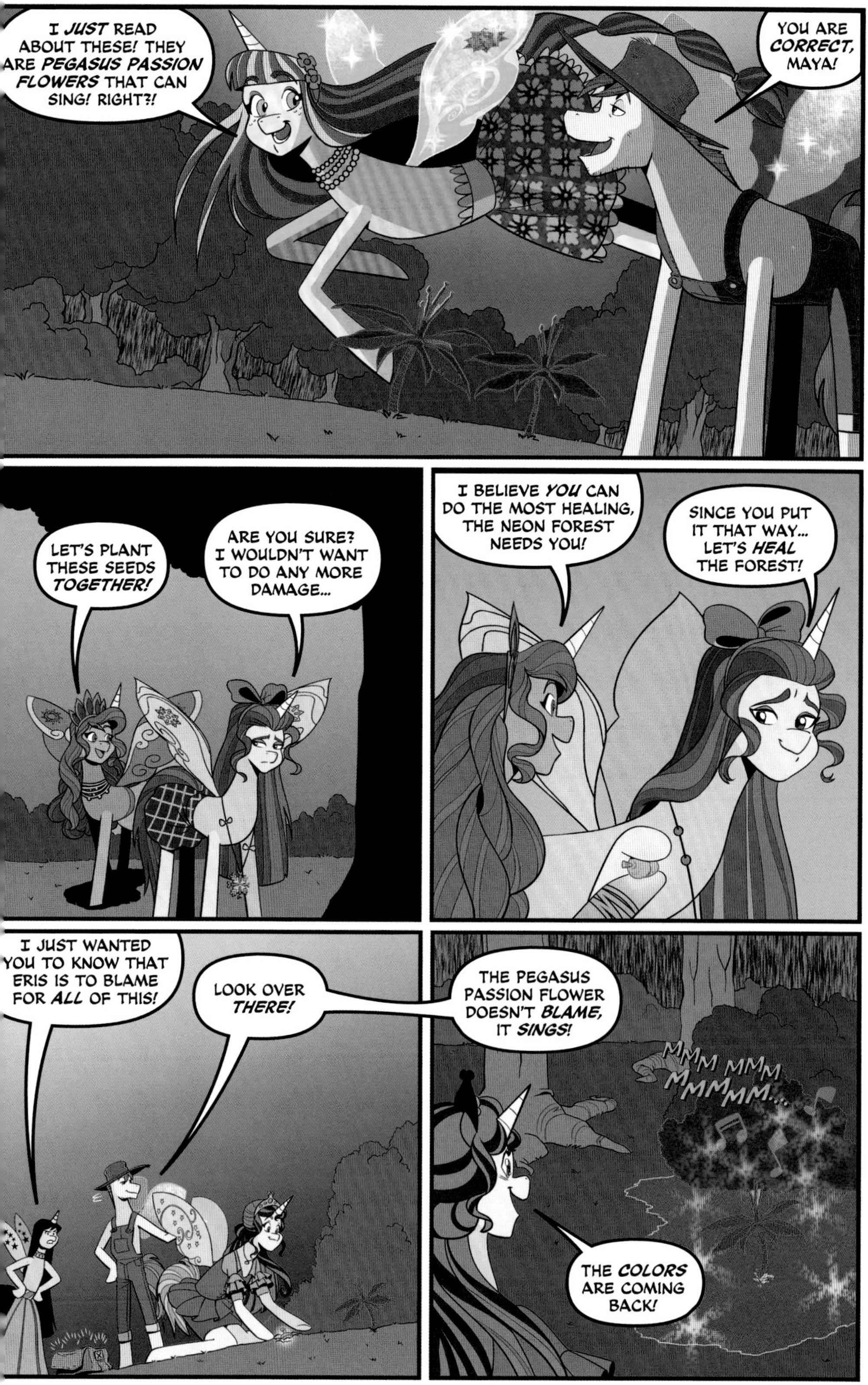
I JUST READ ABOUT THESE! THEY ARE PEGASUS PASSION FLOWERS THAT CAN SING! RIGHT?!
YOU ARE CORRECT, MAYA!
LET'S PLANT THESE SEEDS TOGETHER!
ARE YOU SURE? I WOULDN'T WANT TO DO ANY MORE DAMAGE...
I BELIEVE YOU CAN DO THE MOST HEALING, THE NEON FOREST NEEDS YOU!
SINCE YOU PUT IT THAT WAY... LET'S HEAL THE FOREST!
I JUST WANTED YOU TO KNOW THAT ERIS IS TO BLAME FOR ALL OF THIS!
LOOK OVER THERE!
THE PEGASUS PASSION FLOWER DOESN'T BLAME, IT SINGS!
MMM MMM MMMMM...
THE COLORS ARE COMING BACK!

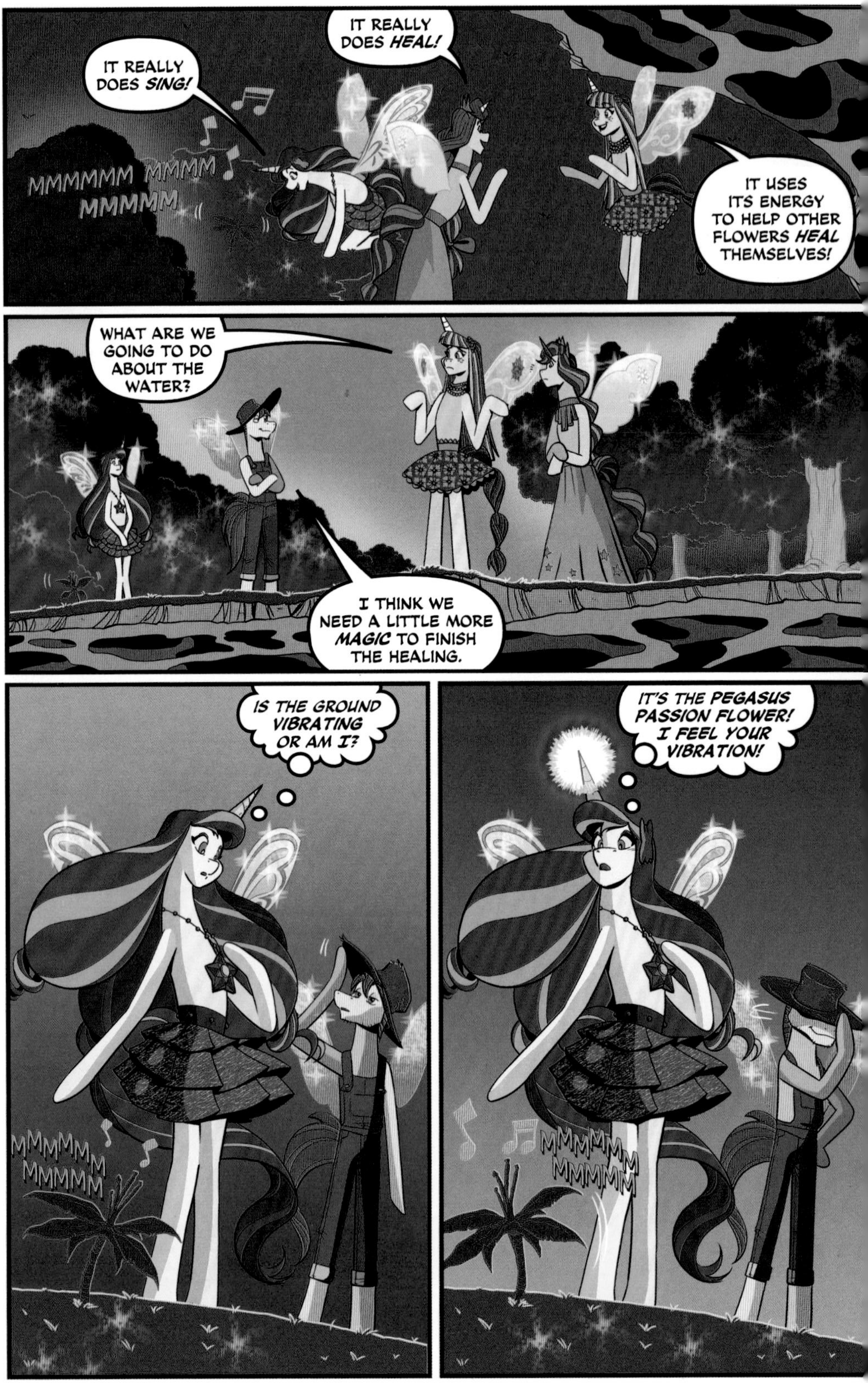
IT REALLY DOES SING!
MMMMMM MMMM MMMMM
IT REALLY DOES HEAL!
IT USES ITS ENERGY TO HELP OTHER FLOWERS HEAL THEMSELVES!
WHAT ARE WE GOING TO DO ABOUT THE WATER?
I THINK WE NEED A LITTLE MORE MAGIC TO FINISH THE HEALING.
IS THE GROUND VIBRATING OR AM I?
MMMMMM MMMMM
IT'S THE PEGASUS PASSION FLOWER! I FEEL YOUR VIBRATION!
MMMMMM MMMMM

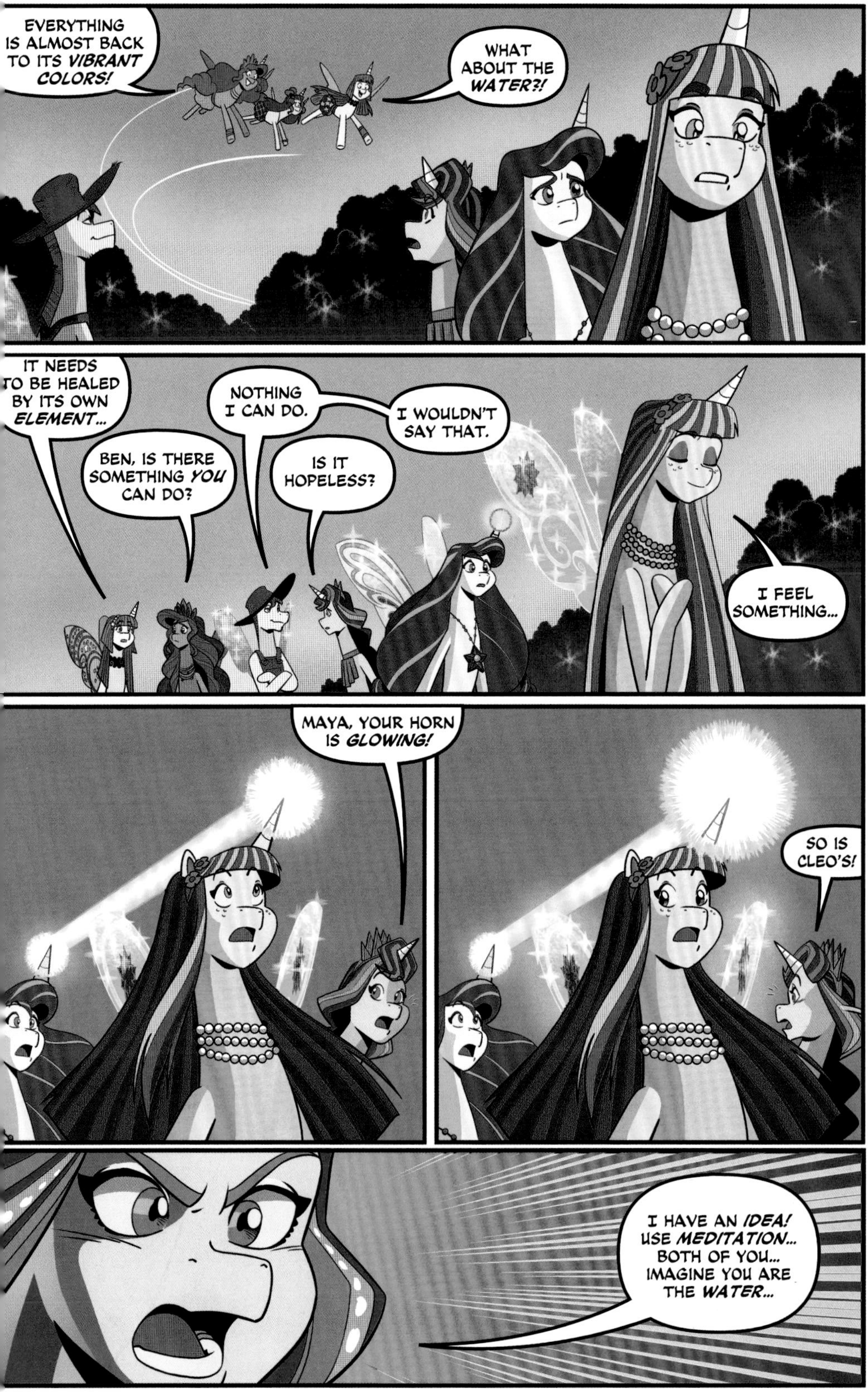
EVERYTHING IS ALMOST BACK TO ITS VIBRANT COLORS!
WHAT ABOUT THE WATER?!
IT NEEDS TO BE HEALED BY ITS OWN ELEMENT...
BEN, IS THERE SOMETHING YOU CAN DO?
NOTHING I CAN DO.
IS IT HOPELESS?
I WOULDN'T SAY THAT.
I FEEL SOMETHING...
MAYA, YOUR HORN IS GLOWING!
SO IS CLEO'S!
I HAVE AN IDEA! USE MEDITATION... BOTH OF YOU... IMAGINE YOU ARE THE WATER...

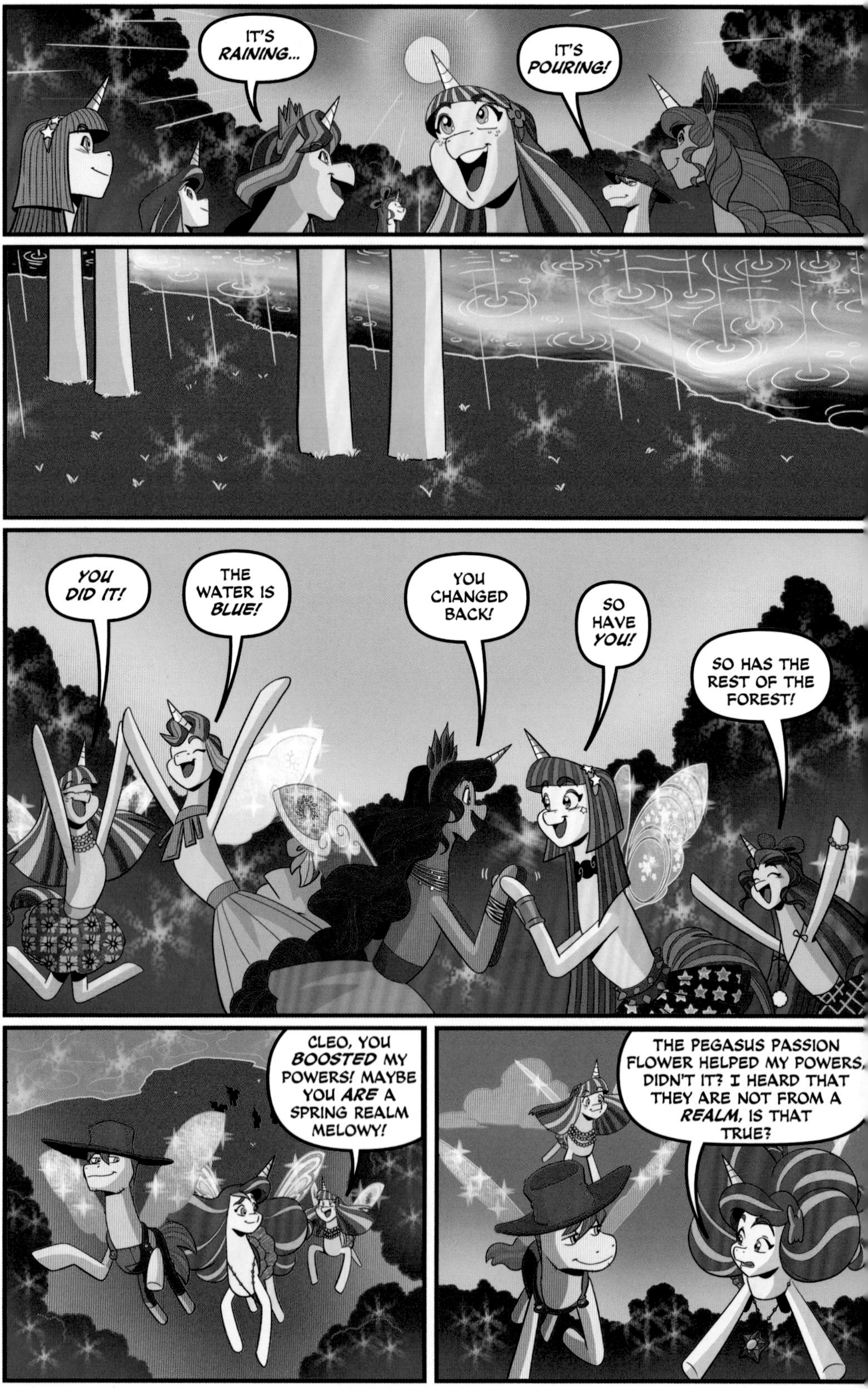
IT'S RAINING...
IT'S POURING!
YOU DID IT!
THE WATER IS BLUE!
YOU CHANGED BACK!
SO HAVE YOU!
SO HAS THE REST OF THE FOREST!
CLEO, YOU BOOSTED MY POWERS! MAYBE YOU ARE A SPRING REALM MELOWY!
THE PEGASUS PASSION FLOWER HELPED MY POWERS, DIDN'T IT? I HEARD THAT THEY ARE NOT FROM A REALM, IS THAT TRUE?

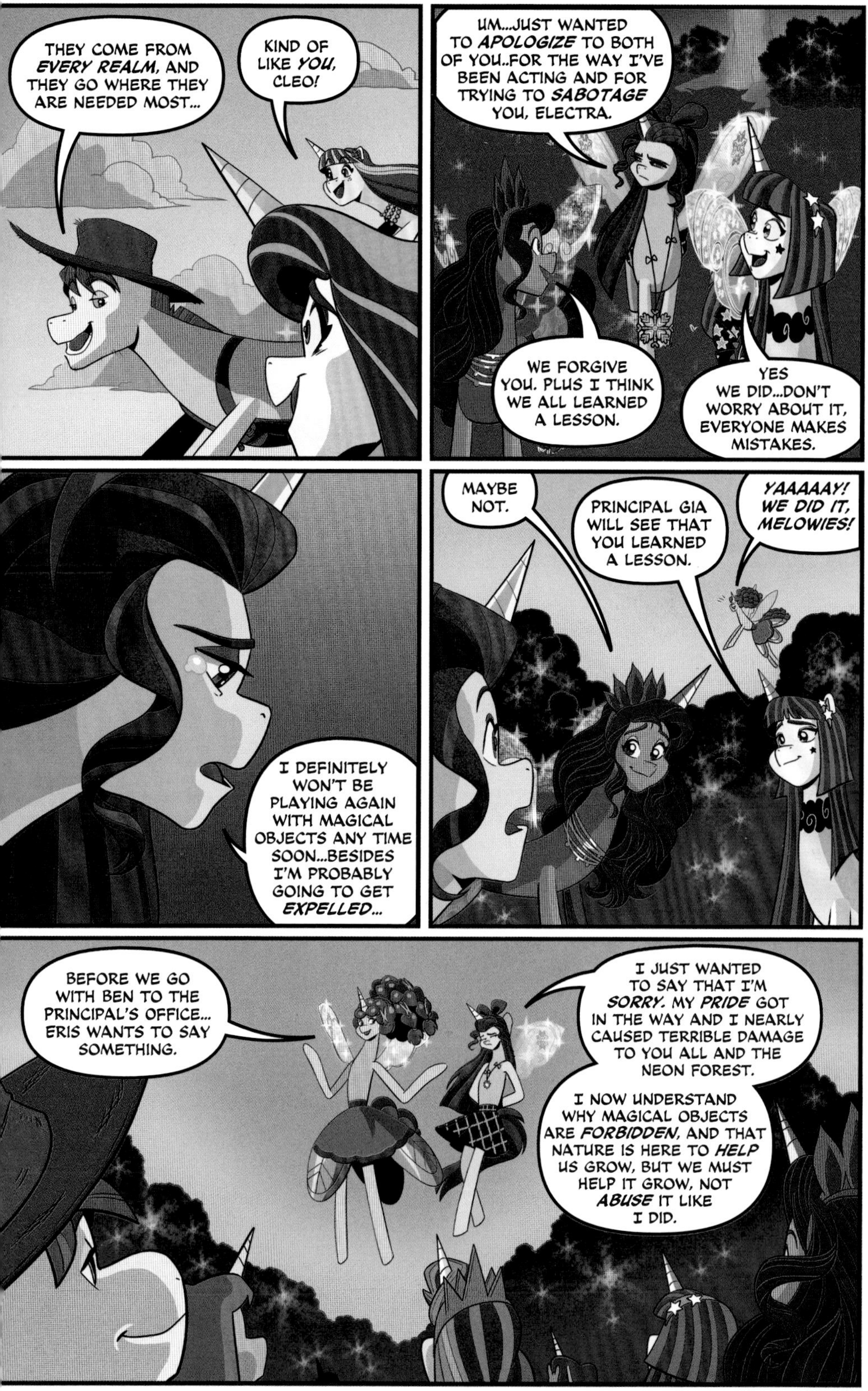
THEY COME FROM EVERY REALM, AND THEY GO WHERE THEY ARE NEEDED MOST...
KIND OF LIKE YOU, CLEO!
UM...JUST WANTED TO APOLOGIZE TO BOTH OF YOU..FOR THE WAY I'VE BEEN ACTING AND FOR TRYING TO SABOTAGE YOU, ELECTRA.
WE FORGIVE YOU. PLUS I THINK WE ALL LEARNED A LESSON.
YES WE DID...DON'T WORRY ABOUT IT, EVERYONE MAKES MISTAKES.
I DEFINITELY WON'T BE PLAYING AGAIN WITH MAGICAL OBJECTS ANY TIME SOON...BESIDES I'M PROBABLY GOING TO GET EXPELLED...
MAYBE NOT.
PRINCIPAL GIA WILL SEE THAT YOU LEARNED A LESSON.
YAAAAAY! WE DID IT, MELOWIES!
BEFORE WE GO WITH BEN TO THE PRINCIPAL'S OFFICE... ERIS WANTS TO SAY SOMETHING.
I JUST WANTED TO SAY THAT I'M SORRY. MY PRIDE GOT IN THE WAY AND I NEARLY CAUSED TERRIBLE DAMAGE TO YOU ALL AND THE NEON FOREST.
I NOW UNDERSTAND WHY MAGICAL OBJECTS ARE FORBIDDEN, AND THAT NATURE IS HERE TO HELP US GROW, BUT WE MUST HELP IT GROW, NOT ABUSE IT LIKE I DID.

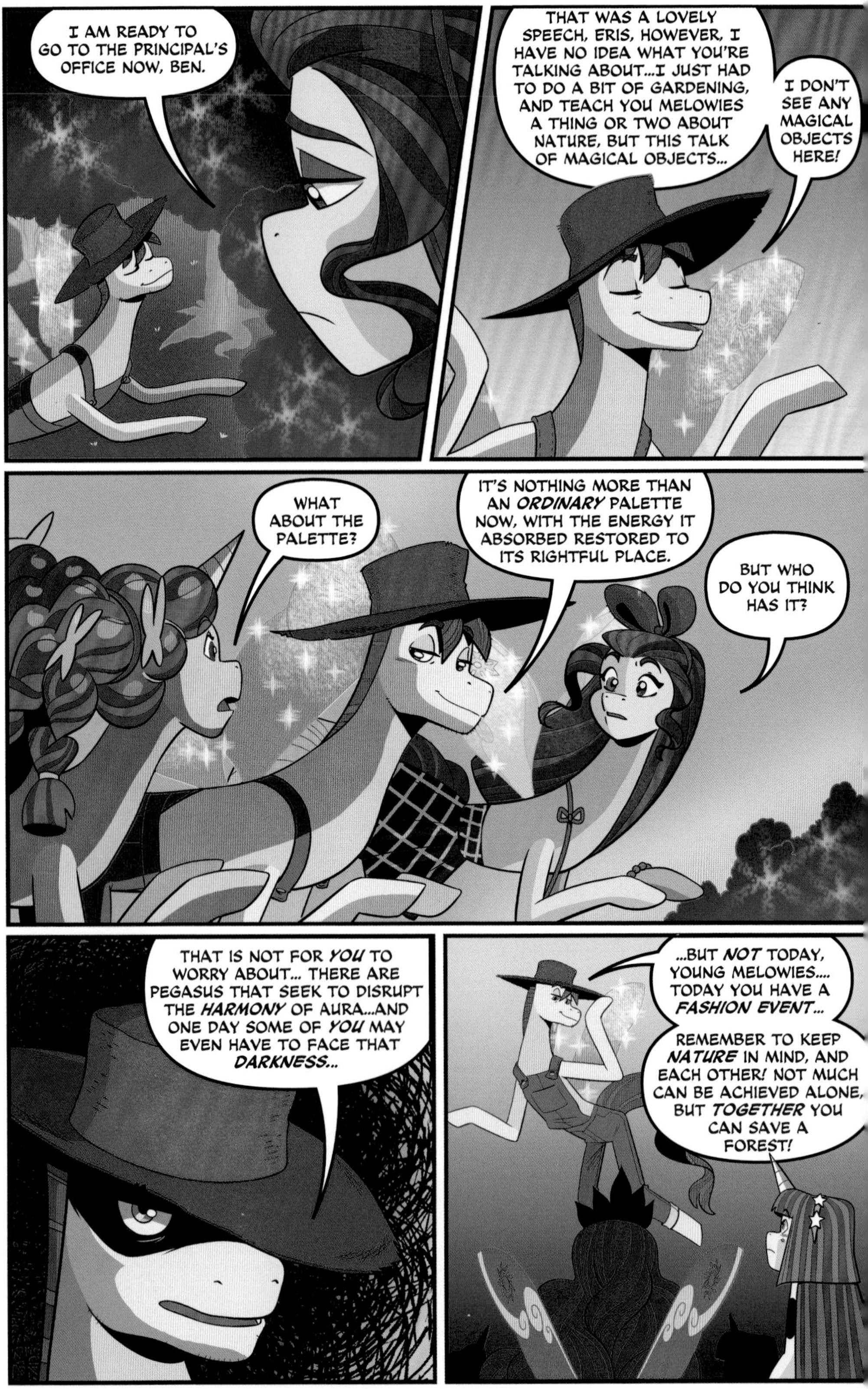

I AM READY TO GO TO THE PRINCIPAL'S OFFICE NOW, BEN.
THAT WAS A LOVELY SPEECH, ERIS, HOWEVER, I HAVE NO IDEA WHAT YOU'RE TALKING ABOUT...I JUST HAD TO DO A BIT OF GARDENING, AND TEACH YOU MELOWIES A THING OR TWO ABOUT NATURE, BUT THIS TALK OF MAGICAL OBJECTS...
I DON'T SEE ANY MAGICAL OBJECTS HERE!
WHAT ABOUT THE PALETTE?
IT'S NOTHING MORE THAN AN *ORDINARY* PALETTE NOW, WITH THE ENERGY IT ABSORBED RESTORED TO ITS RIGHTFUL PLACE.
BUT WHO DO YOU THINK HAS IT?
THAT IS NOT FOR *YOU* TO WORRY ABOUT... THERE ARE PEGASUS THAT SEEK TO DISRUPT THE *HARMONY* OF AURA...AND ONE DAY SOME OF *YOU* MAY EVEN HAVE TO FACE THAT *DARKNESS...*
...BUT *NOT* TODAY, YOUNG MELOWIES.... TODAY YOU HAVE A *FASHION EVENT...*
REMEMBER TO KEEP *NATURE* IN MIND, AND EACH OTHER! NOT MUCH CAN BE ACHIEVED ALONE, BUT *TOGETHER* YOU CAN SAVE A FOREST!

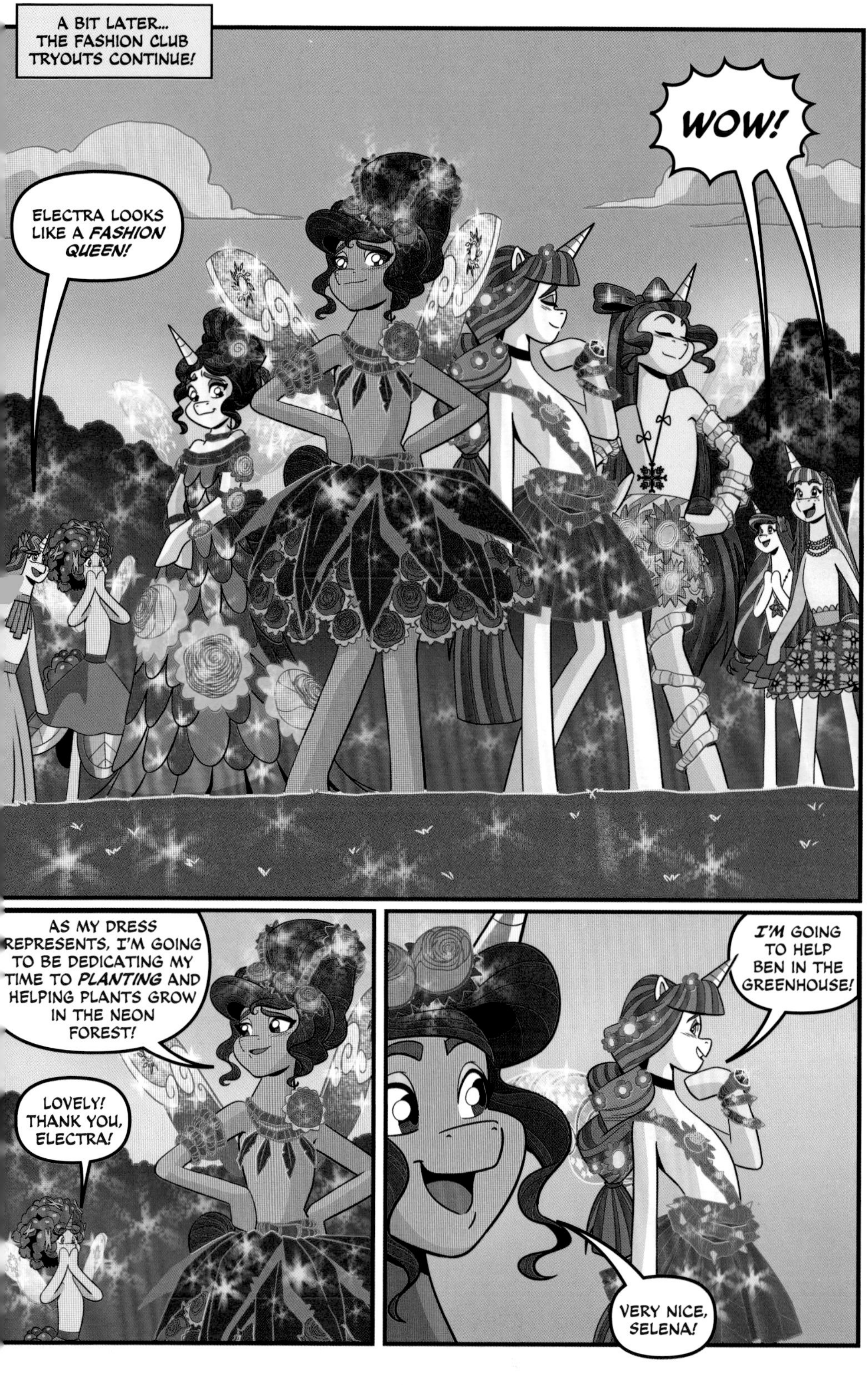
A BIT LATER... THE FASHION CLUB TRYOUTS CONTINUE!
WOW!
ELECTRA LOOKS LIKE A *FASHION QUEEN!*
AS MY DRESS REPRESENTS, I'M GOING TO BE DEDICATING MY TIME TO *PLANTING* AND HELPING PLANTS GROW IN THE NEON FOREST!
LOVELY! THANK YOU, ELECTRA!
I'M GOING TO HELP BEN IN THE GREENHOUSE!
VERY NICE, SELENA!

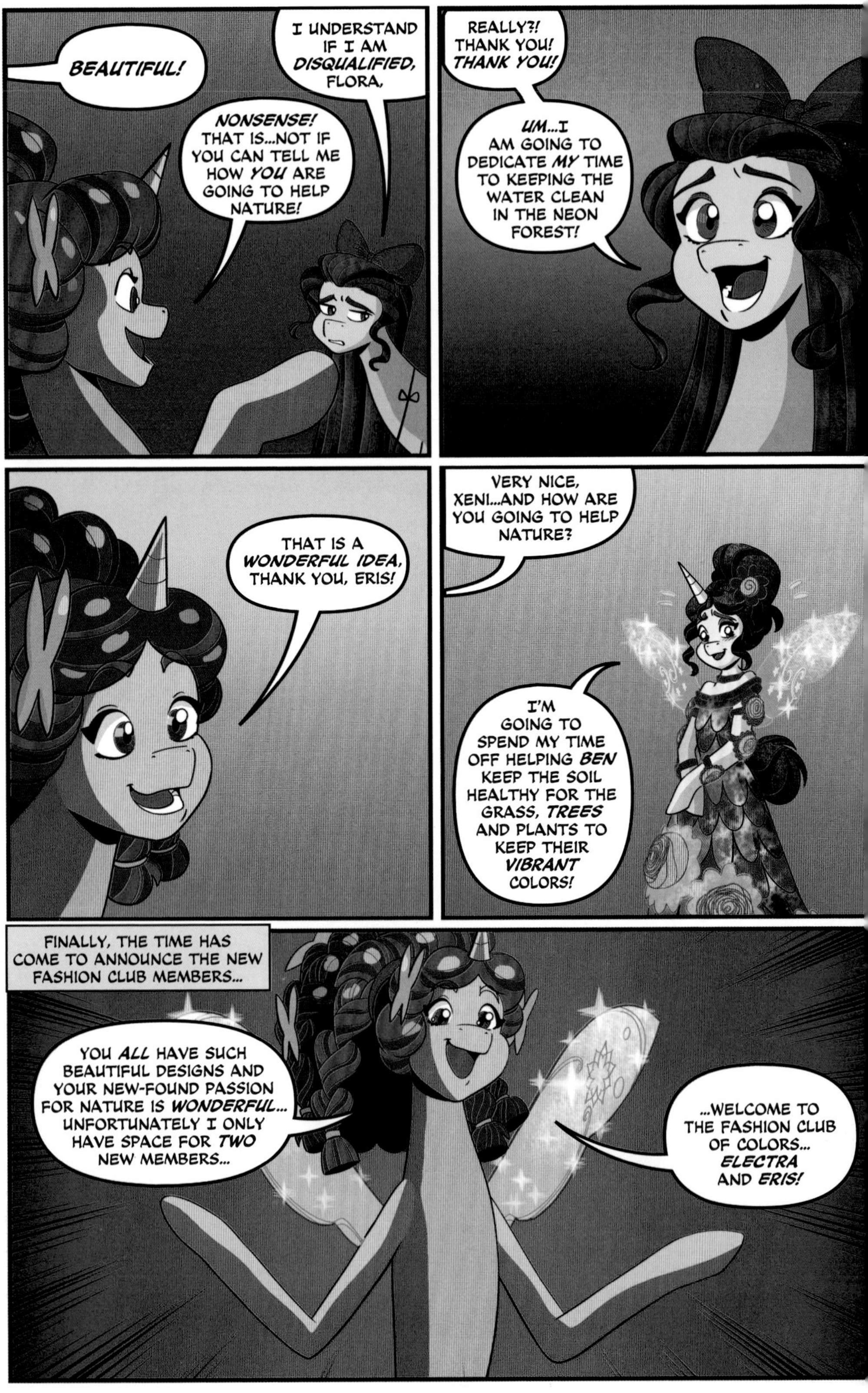
BEAUTIFUL!
I UNDERSTAND IF I AM DISQUALIFIED, FLORA,
NONSENSE! THAT IS...NOT IF YOU CAN TELL ME HOW YOU ARE GOING TO HELP NATURE!
REALLY?! THANK YOU! THANK YOU!
UM...I AM GOING TO DEDICATE MY TIME TO KEEPING THE WATER CLEAN IN THE NEON FOREST!
THAT IS A WONDERFUL IDEA, THANK YOU, ERIS!
VERY NICE, XENI...AND HOW ARE YOU GOING TO HELP NATURE?
I'M GOING TO SPEND MY TIME OFF HELPING BEN KEEP THE SOIL HEALTHY FOR THE GRASS, TREES AND PLANTS TO KEEP THEIR VIBRANT COLORS!
FINALLY, THE TIME HAS COME TO ANNOUNCE THE NEW FASHION CLUB MEMBERS...
YOU ALL HAVE SUCH BEAUTIFUL DESIGNS AND YOUR NEW-FOUND PASSION FOR NATURE IS WONDERFUL... UNFORTUNATELY I ONLY HAVE SPACE FOR TWO NEW MEMBERS...
...WELCOME TO THE FASHION CLUB OF COLORS... ELECTRA AND ERIS!

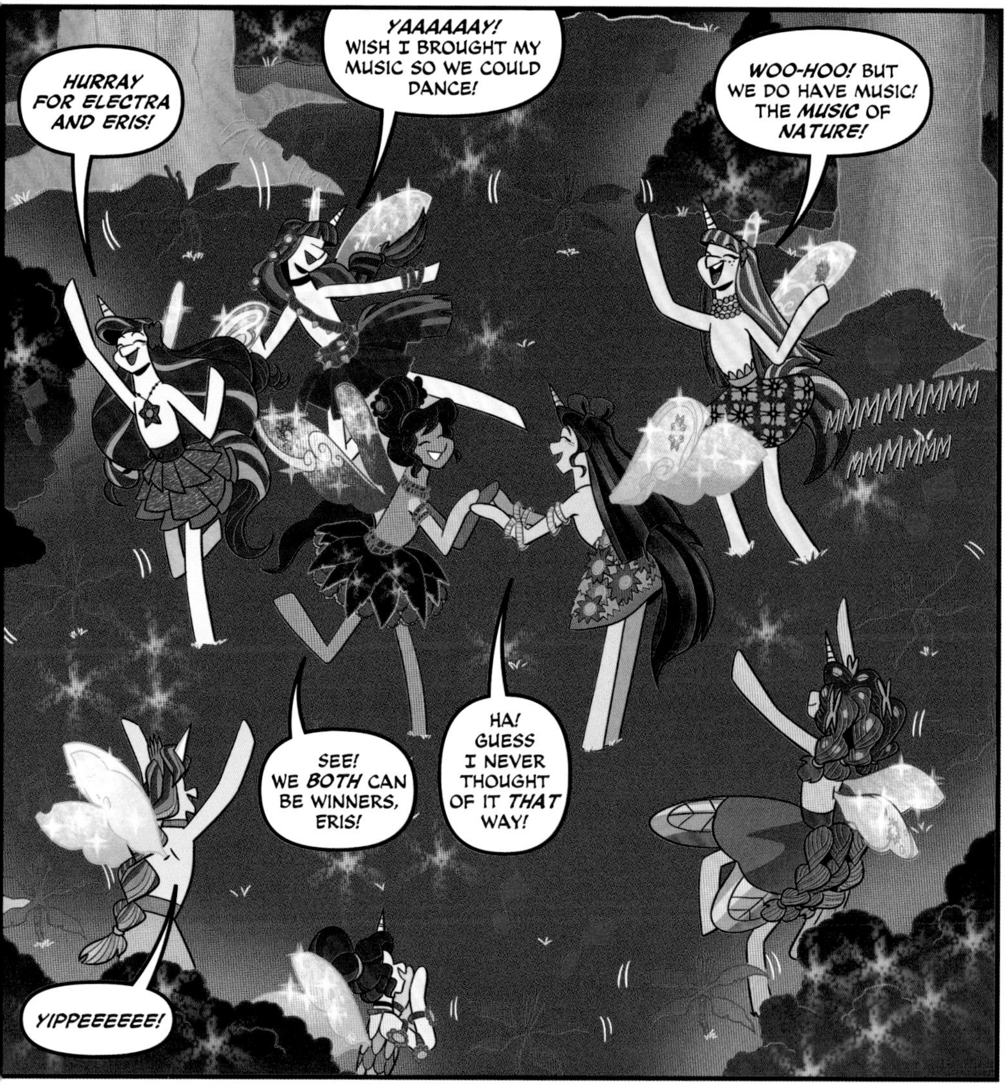
HURRAY FOR ELECTRA AND ERIS!
YAAAAAAY! WISH I BROUGHT MY MUSIC SO WE COULD DANCE!
WOO-HOO! BUT WE DO HAVE MUSIC! THE MUSIC OF NATURE!
MMMMMMMMM MMMMMMM
SEE! WE BOTH CAN BE WINNERS, ERIS!
HA! GUESS I NEVER THOUGHT OF IT THAT WAY!
YIPPEEEEEEE!

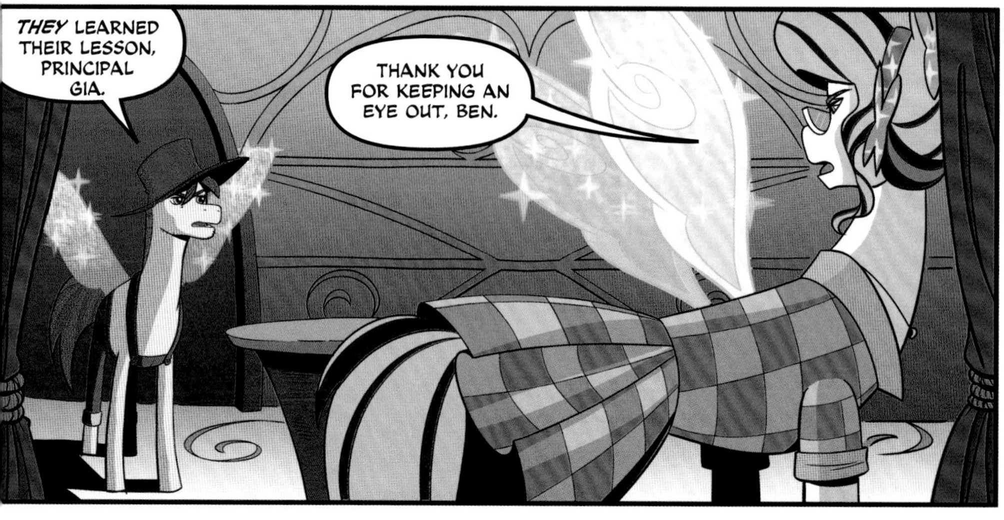
THEY LEARNED THEIR LESSON, PRINCIPAL GIA.
THANK YOU FOR KEEPING AN EYE OUT, BEN.

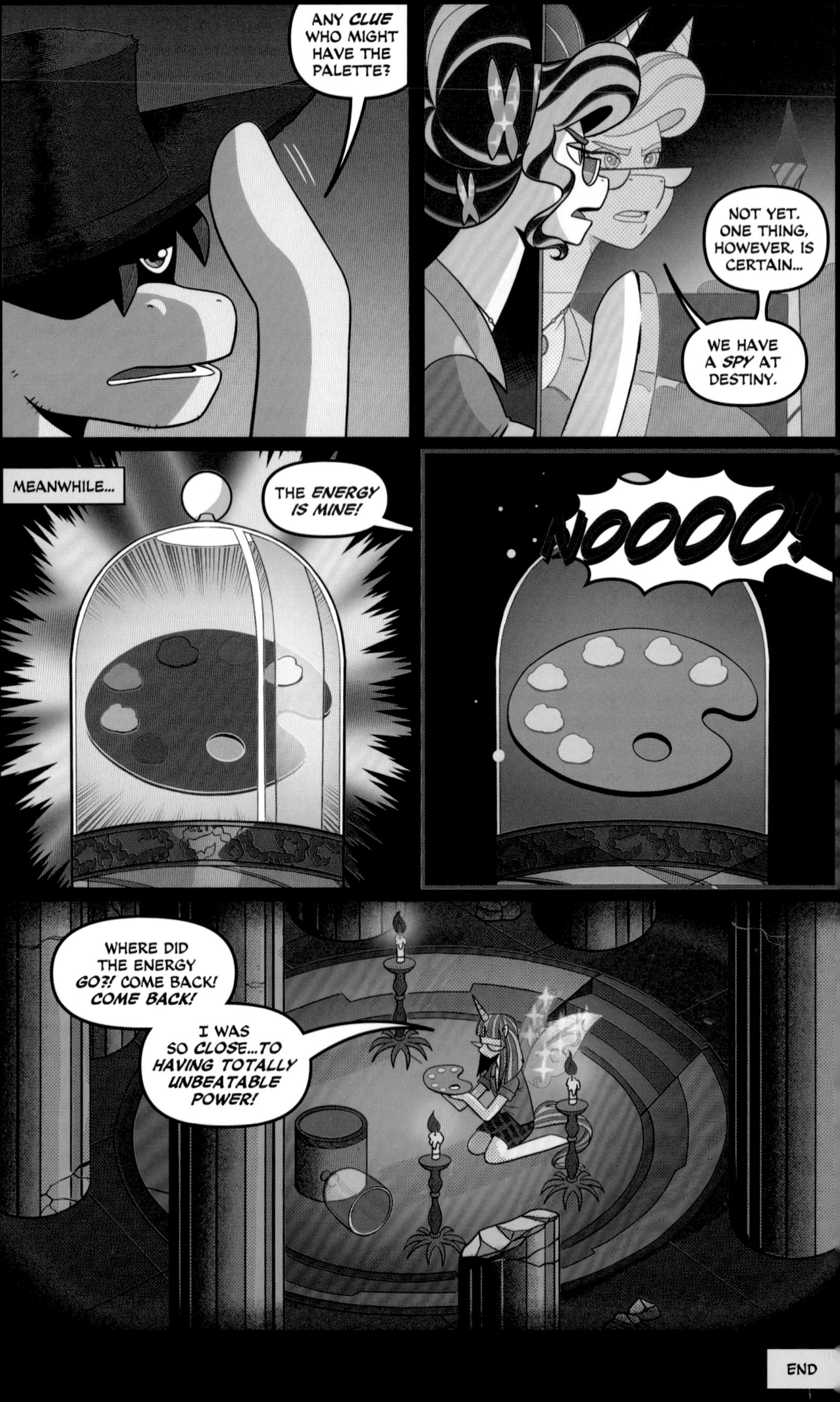
ANY CLUE WHO MIGHT HAVE THE PALETTE?
NOT YET. ONE THING, HOWEVER, IS CERTAIN...
WE HAVE A SPY AT DESTINY.
MEANWHILE...
THE ENERGY IS MINE!
NOOOO!
WHERE DID THE ENERGY GO?! COME BACK! COME BACK!
I WAS SO CLOSE...TO HAVING TOTALLY UNBEATABLE POWER!
END

WATCH OUT FOR PAPERCUTZ™

Welcome to the sparkly, second MELOWY graphic novel by Cortney Powell and Ryan Jampole based on the characters created by Danielle Star, magically brought to you by Papercutz, those enchanting folks dedicated to publishing graphic novels for all ages. I'm Jim Salicrup, the Editor-in-Chief and a Fashion Club reject, here to offer peeks into what's happening in the wonderful world of Papercutz, and maybe even offer a little behind-the-scenes info regarding the creators that bring you the MELOWY graphic novels...

MELOWY was created by the fascinating Danielle Star, and she's also the author of the chapter books published by our good friends at Scholastic. Danielle Star has done a bit of everything. She's been an assistant cook at a famous French pastry shop, the head editor of a fashion magazine, and a dance teacher. Once she started writing, though, she never stopped. Today she lives in the English countryside with her five horses, her cat Sugar Cube, and her dog Fluffy. Every morning before she starts writing, she drinks a big wild strawberry smoothie and reads a good book.

Cortney Powell

It's funny, when I think about Danielle Star's bio, she reminds me of so many characters that we just happen to publish at Papercutz! For example, she was an assistant cook at a famous French pastry shop, and that makes me think of SWEETIES, a series published by our Charmz imprint, and based on *The Chocolate Box Girls* books by Cathy Cassidy. The series is about a recently blended family, where the dad works as a candy-maker. Danielle was also involved in the world of fashion, something of great interest to BARBIE in her Papercutz graphic novels. She also was a dance teacher, and need I mention that we publish the wonderful DANCE CLASS graphic novels by Bêka and Crip? But when I saw that Danielle has five horses and a dog named Fluffy...well, I think I'm beginning to see where she might come up with ideas for some of her characters.

Cortney Powell, the writer of the MELOWY graphic novels was born in Alabama, but lived most of her life in the magical realm of New York City. Cortney is a writer, poet, actress, filmmaker, animal-lover, and yogini. At an early age Cortney met Batman co-creator Bob Kane and filmmakers Francis Ford Coppola and Lloyd Kaufman at the San Diego Comic-Con. At the prestigious Professional Performing Arts School, she was proud to star as Enid in cartoonist/playwright Linda Barry's play "The Good Times Are Killing Me." A fan of such

comics as BARBIE, LENORE, and LITTLE LULU, Cortney worked on revising the DISNEY FAIRIES scripts for an American audience for the Papercutz graphic novels. Her magical comics journey continues as the writer on the MELOWY graphic novel series, where she believes the most powerful magic of all is: Love.

A yogini, eh? That may offer some insights into why Cora is practicing meditation techniques!

As for MELOWY artist Ryan Jampole, he's quite an accomplished comicbook artist, and has even been nominated for the prestigious Harvey Award, one of the highest honors in the field. Ryan hails from Queens, New York, and attended the High School of Art & Design and the Fashion Institute of Technology—which explains why the fashions showcased by the fashion club were so impressive! Among Ryan's many comics credits, he has drawn MEGAMAN and SONIC for Archie Comics, DEXTER'S LABORATORY and CODENAME KND for IDW, and GEEKY F@B 5, GERONIMO STILTON and THEA STILTON graphic novels for Papercutz.

Ryan Jampole

Speaking of THEA STILTON, we want to mention that her Papercutz graphic novels are being collected in the exciting 3 IN 1 format that's become the latest sensation! It's a simple concept, each 3 IN 1 book collects three entire Papercutz graphic novels into one great big Papercutz graphic novel. In MELOWY #1, we offered a peek at GERONIMO STILTON 3 IN 1 #1, now we'd like to offer a peek into THEA STILTON 3 IN 1 #1 starting on the very next page.

Any discussion of our MELOWY graphic novel creators should also include colorist Laurie E. Smith and letterer Wilson Ramos Jr., but we're running out of room, so we'll have to save their exciting bios until MELOWY #3 "Time to Fly."

Thanks,
Jim

STAY IN TOUCH!

EMAIL: salicrup@papercutz.com
WEB: papercutz.com
TWITTER: @papercutzgn
INSTAGRAM: @papercutzgn
FACEBOOK: PAPERCUTZGRAPHICNOVELS
FANMAIL: Papercutz, 160 Broadway, Suite 700, East Wing, New York, NY 10038

Here's a special preview of THEA STILTON 3 IN 1 #1...

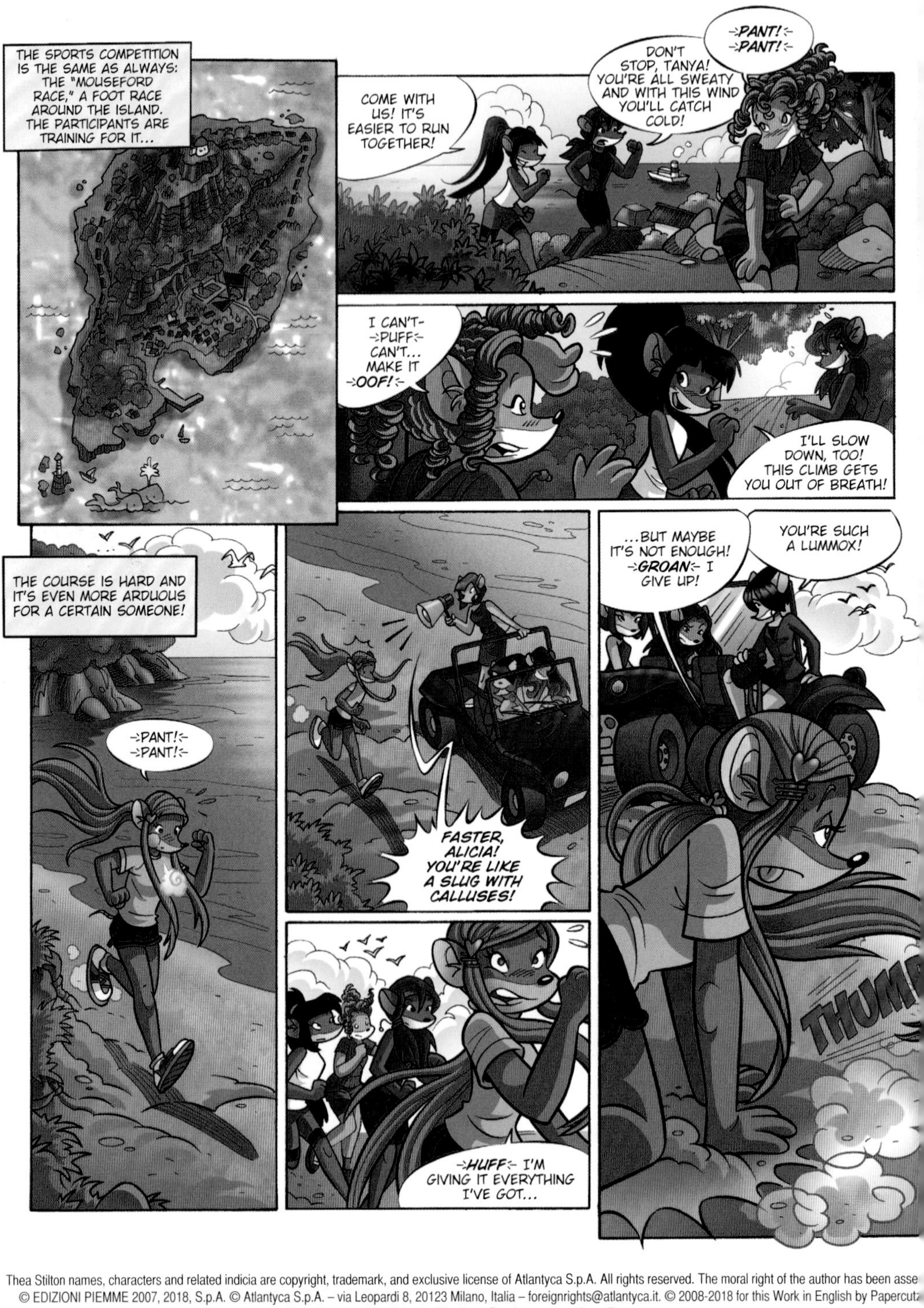
THE SPORTS COMPETITION IS THE SAME AS ALWAYS: THE "MOUSEFORD RACE," A FOOT RACE AROUND THE ISLAND. THE PARTICIPANTS ARE TRAINING FOR IT...
COME WITH US! IT'S EASIER TO RUN TOGETHER!
DON'T STOP, TANYA! YOU'RE ALL SWEATY AND WITH THIS WIND YOU'LL CATCH COLD!
PANT! PANT!
I CAN'T- PUFF- CAN'T... MAKE IT OOF!
I'LL SLOW DOWN, TOO! THIS CLIMB GETS YOU OUT OF BREATH!
THE COURSE IS HARD AND IT'S EVEN MORE ARDUOUS FOR A CERTAIN SOMEONE!
PANT! PANT!
FASTER, ALICIA! YOU'RE LIKE A SLUG WITH CALLUSES!
HUFF I'M GIVING IT EVERYTHING I'VE GOT...
...BUT MAYBE IT'S NOT ENOUGH! GROAN I GIVE UP!
YOU'RE SUCH A LUMMOX!
THUMP

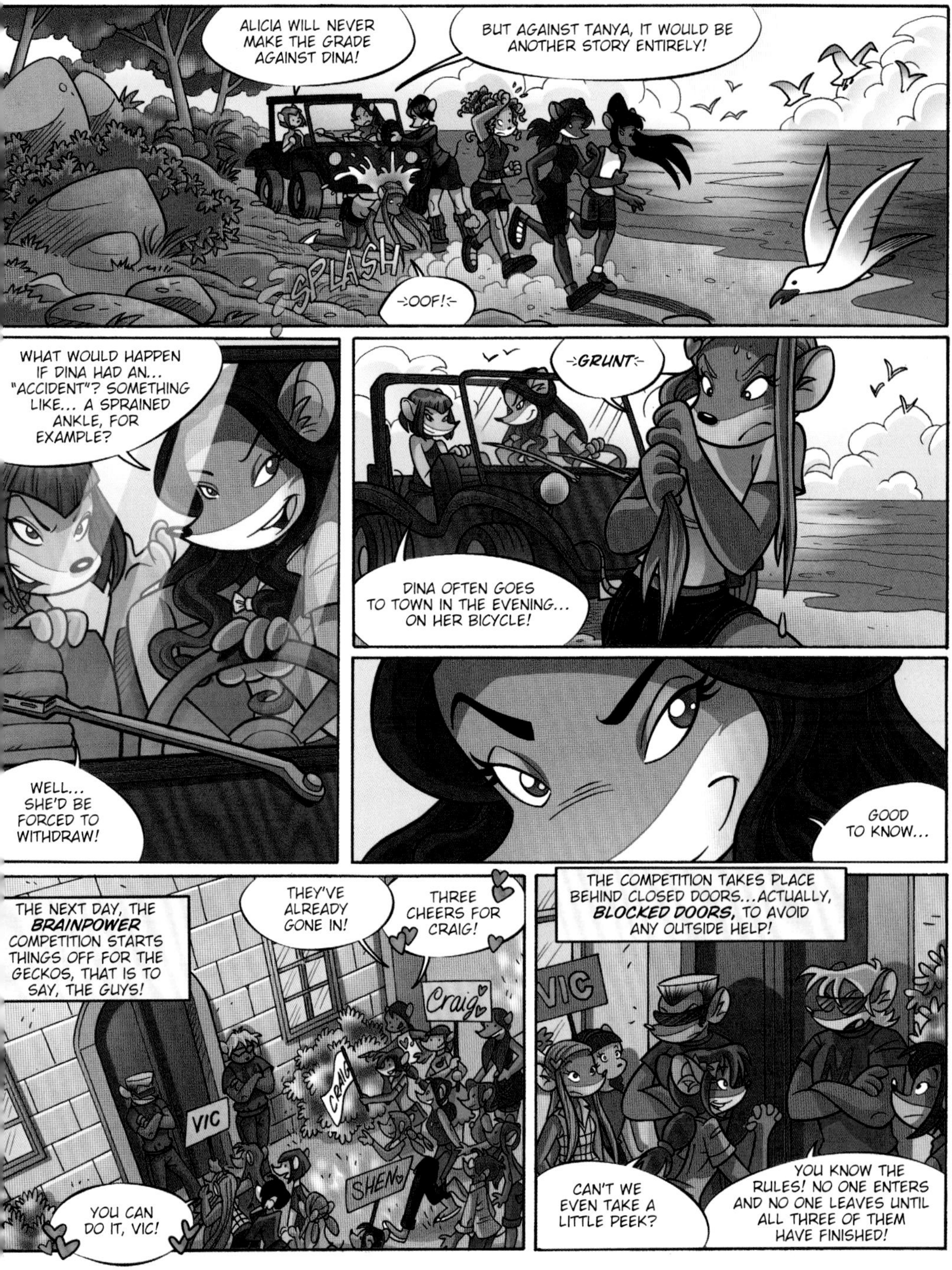
ALICIA WILL NEVER MAKE THE GRADE AGAINST DINA!
BUT AGAINST TANYA, IT WOULD BE ANOTHER STORY ENTIRELY!
SPLASH
OOF!
WHAT WOULD HAPPEN IF DINA HAD AN... "ACCIDENT"? SOMETHING LIKE... A SPRAINED ANKLE, FOR EXAMPLE?
WELL... SHE'D BE FORCED TO WITHDRAW!
GRUNT
DINA OFTEN GOES TO TOWN IN THE EVENING... ON HER BICYCLE!
GOOD TO KNOW...
THE NEXT DAY, THE BRAINPOWER COMPETITION STARTS THINGS OFF FOR THE GECKOS, THAT IS TO SAY, THE GUYS!
THEY'VE ALREADY GONE IN!
THREE CHEERS FOR CRAIG!
Craig
CRAIG
VIC
SHEN
YOU CAN DO IT, VIC!
THE COMPETITION TAKES PLACE BEHIND CLOSED DOORS...ACTUALLY, BLOCKED DOORS, TO AVOID ANY OUTSIDE HELP!
VIC
CAN'T WE EVEN TAKE A LITTLE PEEK?
YOU KNOW THE RULES! NO ONE ENTERS AND NO ONE LEAVES UNTIL ALL THREE OF THEM HAVE FINISHED!

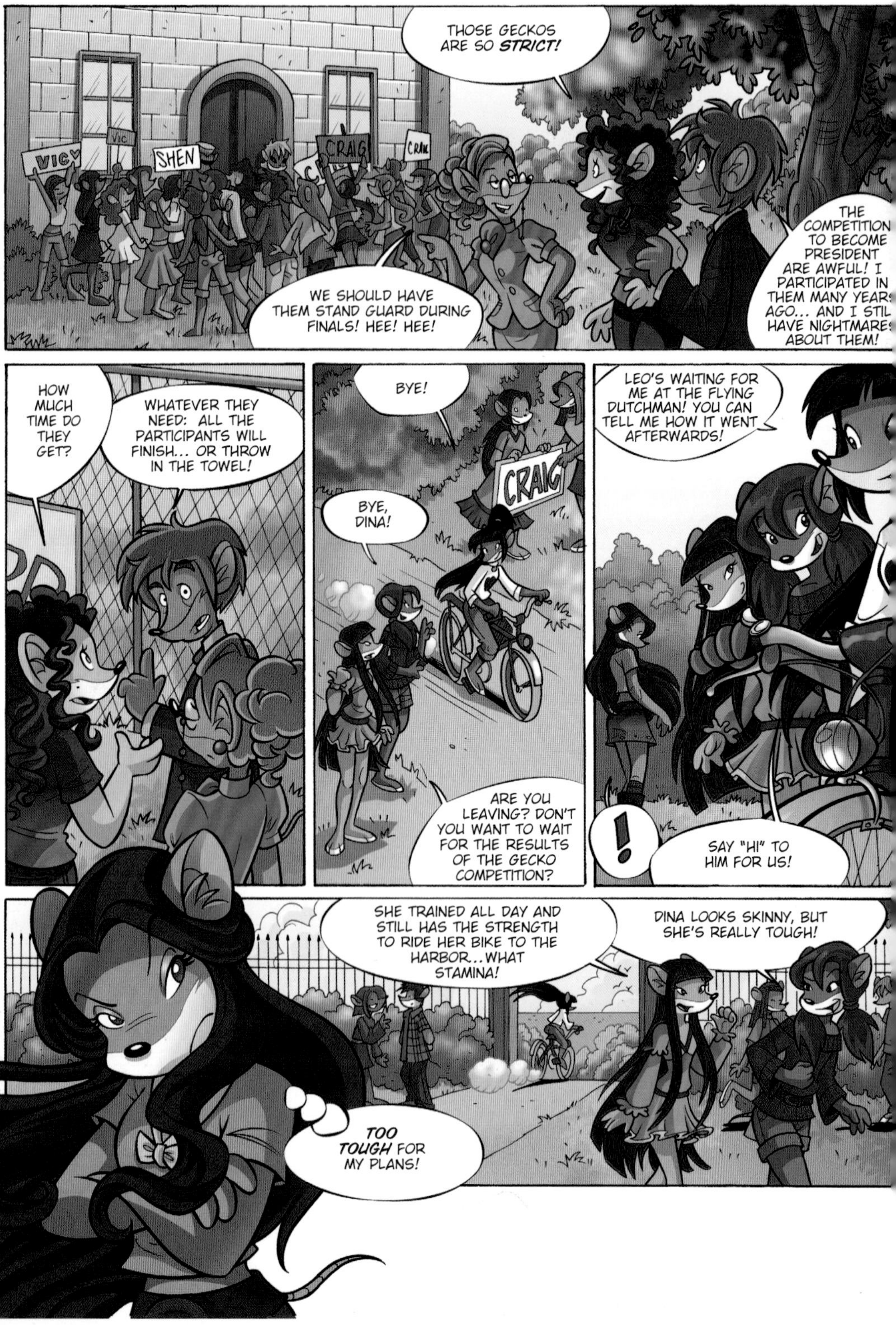
VIC
VIC
SHEN
CRAIG
CRAIG
THOSE GECKOS ARE SO STRICT!
WE SHOULD HAVE THEM STAND GUARD DURING FINALS! HEE! HEE!
THE COMPETITION TO BECOME PRESIDENT ARE AWFUL! I PARTICIPATED IN THEM MANY YEARS AGO... AND I STILL HAVE NIGHTMARES ABOUT THEM!
HOW MUCH TIME DO THEY GET?
WHATEVER THEY NEED: ALL THE PARTICIPANTS WILL FINISH... OR THROW IN THE TOWEL!
BYE!
CRAIG
BYE, DINA!
ARE YOU LEAVING? DON'T YOU WANT TO WAIT FOR THE RESULTS OF THE GECKO COMPETITION?
LEO'S WAITING FOR ME AT THE FLYING DUTCHMAN! YOU CAN TELL ME HOW IT WENT AFTERWARDS!
!
SAY "HI" TO HIM FOR US!
SHE TRAINED ALL DAY AND STILL HAS THE STRENGTH TO RIDE HER BIKE TO THE HARBOR...WHAT STAMINA!
DINA LOOKS SKINNY, BUT SHE'S REALLY TOUGH!
TOO TOUGH FOR MY PLANS!

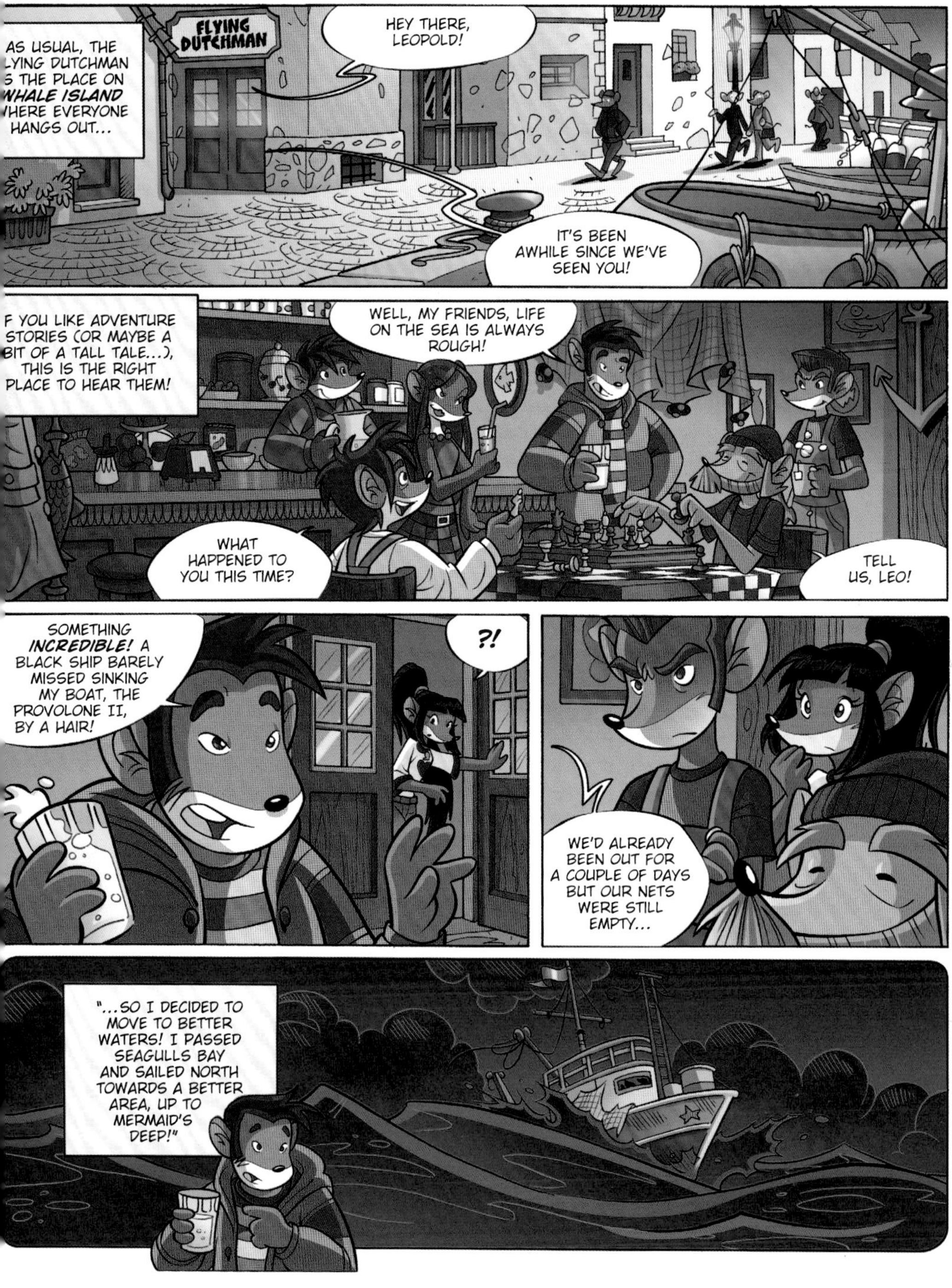
AS USUAL, THE
LYING DUTCHMAN
S THE PLACE ON
WHALE ISLAND
WHERE EVERYONE
HANGS OUT...
FLYING DUTCHMAN
HEY THERE, LEOPOLD!
IT'S BEEN AWHILE SINCE WE'VE SEEN YOU!
F YOU LIKE ADVENTURE STORIES (OR MAYBE A BIT OF A TALL TALE...), THIS IS THE RIGHT PLACE TO HEAR THEM!
WELL, MY FRIENDS, LIFE ON THE SEA IS ALWAYS ROUGH!
WHAT HAPPENED TO YOU THIS TIME?
TELL US, LEO!
SOMETHING INCREDIBLE! A BLACK SHIP BARELY MISSED SINKING MY BOAT, THE PROVOLONE II, BY A HAIR!
?!
WE'D ALREADY BEEN OUT FOR A COUPLE OF DAYS BUT OUR NETS WERE STILL EMPTY...
"...SO I DECIDED TO MOVE TO BETTER WATERS! I PASSED SEAGULLS BAY AND SAILED NORTH TOWARDS A BETTER AREA, UP TO MERMAID'S DEEP!"

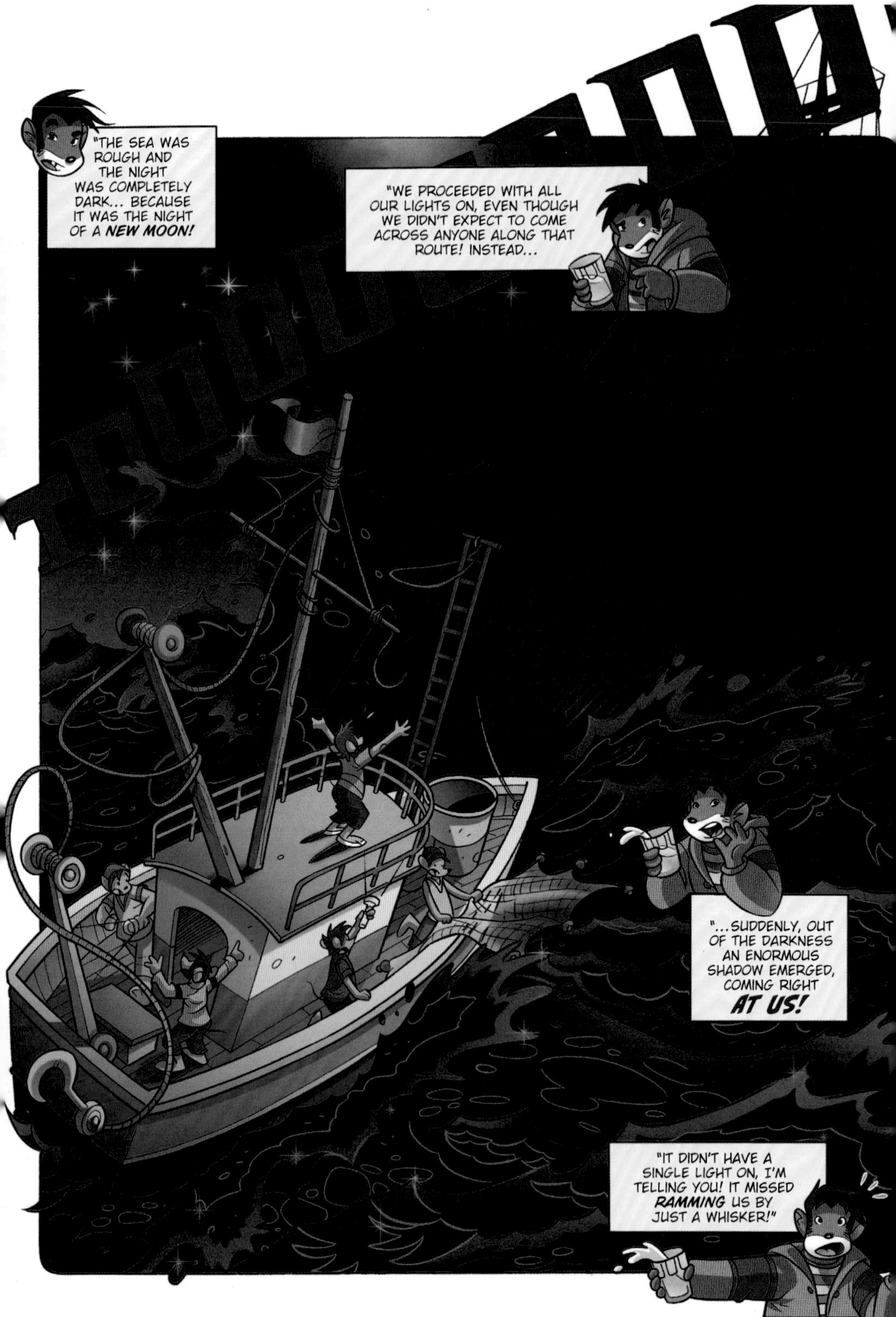
"THE SEA WAS ROUGH AND THE NIGHT WAS COMPLETELY DARK... BECAUSE IT WAS THE NIGHT OF A NEW MOON!
"WE PROCEEDED WITH ALL OUR LIGHTS ON, EVEN THOUGH WE DIDN'T EXPECT TO COME ACROSS ANYONE ALONG THAT ROUTE! INSTEAD...
"...SUDDENLY, OUT OF THE DARKNESS AN ENORMOUS SHADOW EMERGED, COMING RIGHT AT US!
"IT DIDN'T HAVE A SINGLE LIGHT ON, I'M TELLING YOU! IT MISSED RAMMING US BY JUST A WHISKER!"

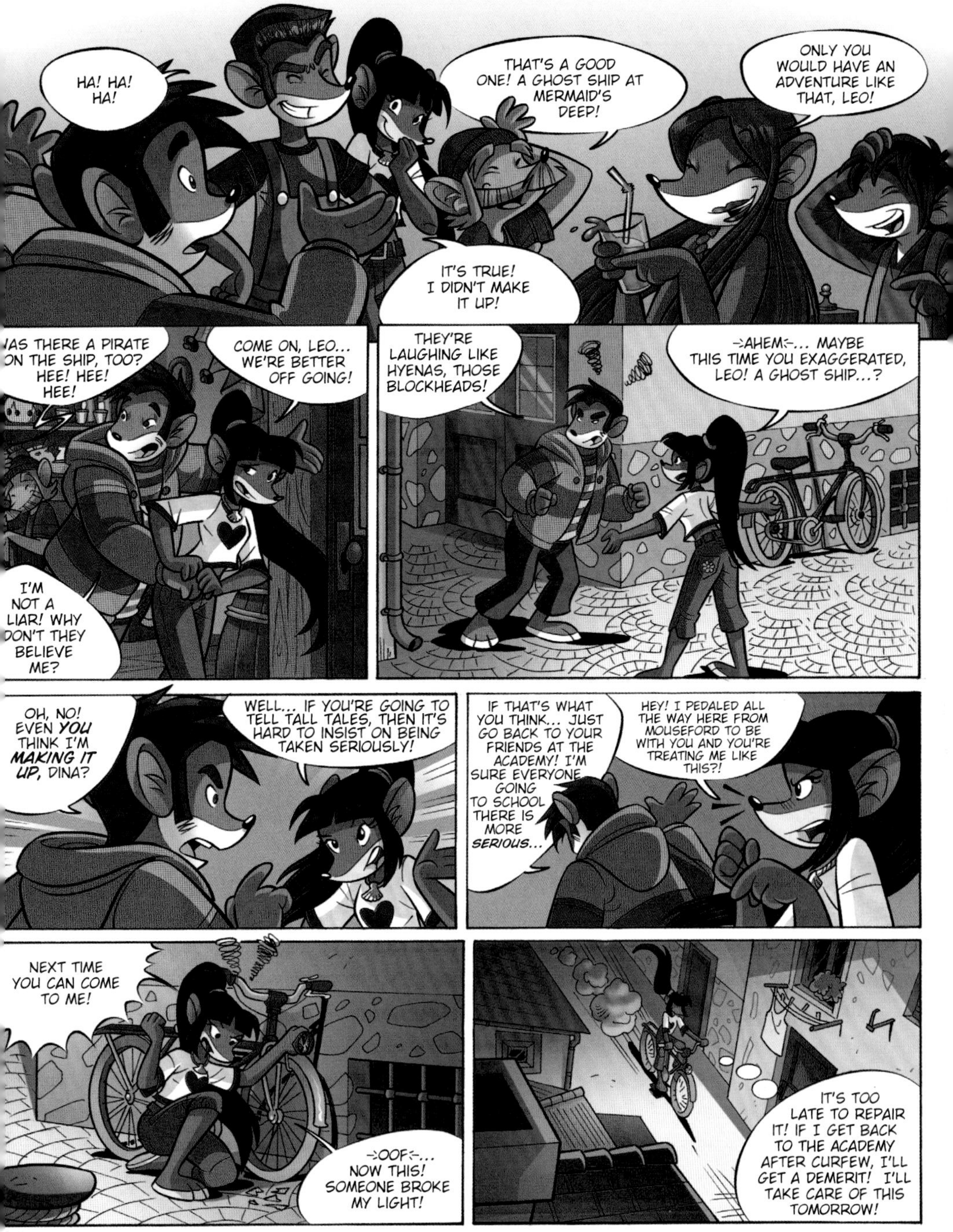
HA! HA! HA!
THAT'S A GOOD ONE! A GHOST SHIP AT MERMAID'S DEEP!
ONLY YOU WOULD HAVE AN ADVENTURE LIKE THAT, LEO!
IT'S TRUE! I DIDN'T MAKE IT UP!
WAS THERE A PIRATE ON THE SHIP, TOO? HEE! HEE! HEE!
COME ON, LEO... WE'RE BETTER OFF GOING!
I'M NOT A LIAR! WHY DON'T THEY BELIEVE ME?
THEY'RE LAUGHING LIKE HYENAS, THOSE BLOCKHEADS!
AHEM... MAYBE THIS TIME YOU EXAGGERATED, LEO! A GHOST SHIP...?
OH, NO! EVEN YOU THINK I'M MAKING IT UP, DINA?
WELL... IF YOU'RE GOING TO TELL TALL TALES, THEN IT'S HARD TO INSIST ON BEING TAKEN SERIOUSLY!
IF THAT'S WHAT YOU THINK... JUST GO BACK TO YOUR FRIENDS AT THE ACADEMY! I'M SURE EVERYONE GOING TO SCHOOL THERE IS MORE SERIOUS...
HEY! I PEDALED ALL THE WAY HERE FROM MOUSEFORD TO BE WITH YOU AND YOU'RE TREATING ME LIKE THIS?!
NEXT TIME YOU CAN COME TO ME!
OOF... NOW THIS! SOMEONE BROKE MY LIGHT!
IT'S TOO LATE TO REPAIR IT! IF I GET BACK TO THE ACADEMY AFTER CURFEW, I'LL GET A DEMERIT! I'LL TAKE CARE OF THIS TOMORROW!

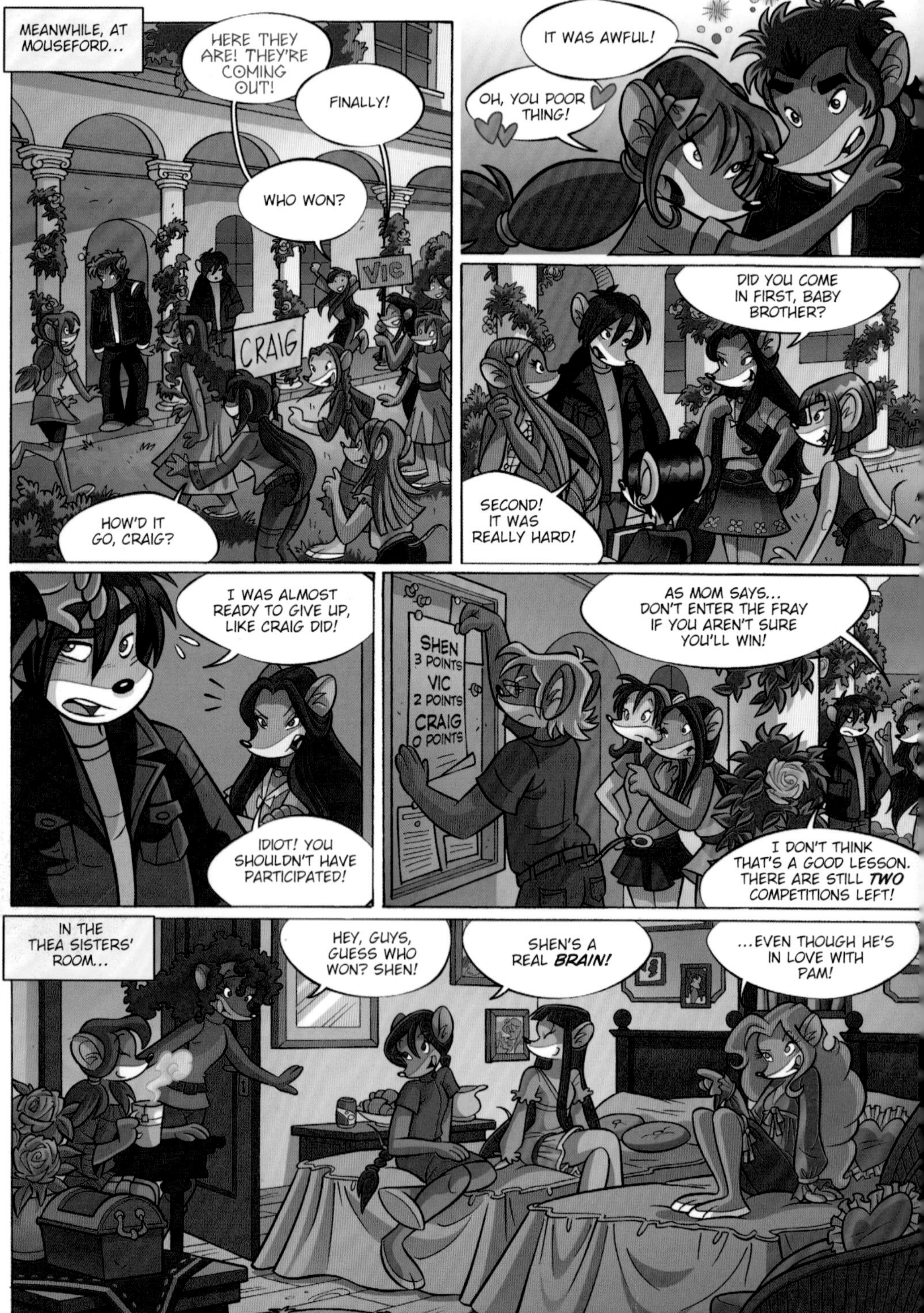
MEANWHILE, AT MOUSEFORD...
HERE THEY ARE! THEY'RE COMING OUT!
FINALLY!
WHO WON?
VIC
CRAIG
HOW'D IT GO, CRAIG?
IT WAS AWFUL!
OH, YOU POOR THING!
DID YOU COME IN FIRST, BABY BROTHER?
SECOND! IT WAS REALLY HARD!
I WAS ALMOST READY TO GIVE UP, LIKE CRAIG DID!
IDIOT! YOU SHOULDN'T HAVE PARTICIPATED!
SHEN 3 POINTS VIC 2 POINTS CRAIG 0 POINTS
AS MOM SAYS... DON'T ENTER THE FRAY IF YOU AREN'T SURE YOU'LL WIN!
I DON'T THINK THAT'S A GOOD LESSON. THERE ARE STILL TWO COMPETITIONS LEFT!
IN THE THEA SISTERS' ROOM...
HEY, GUYS, GUESS WHO WON? SHEN!
SHEN'S A REAL BRAIN!
...EVEN THOUGH HE'S IN LOVE WITH PAM!

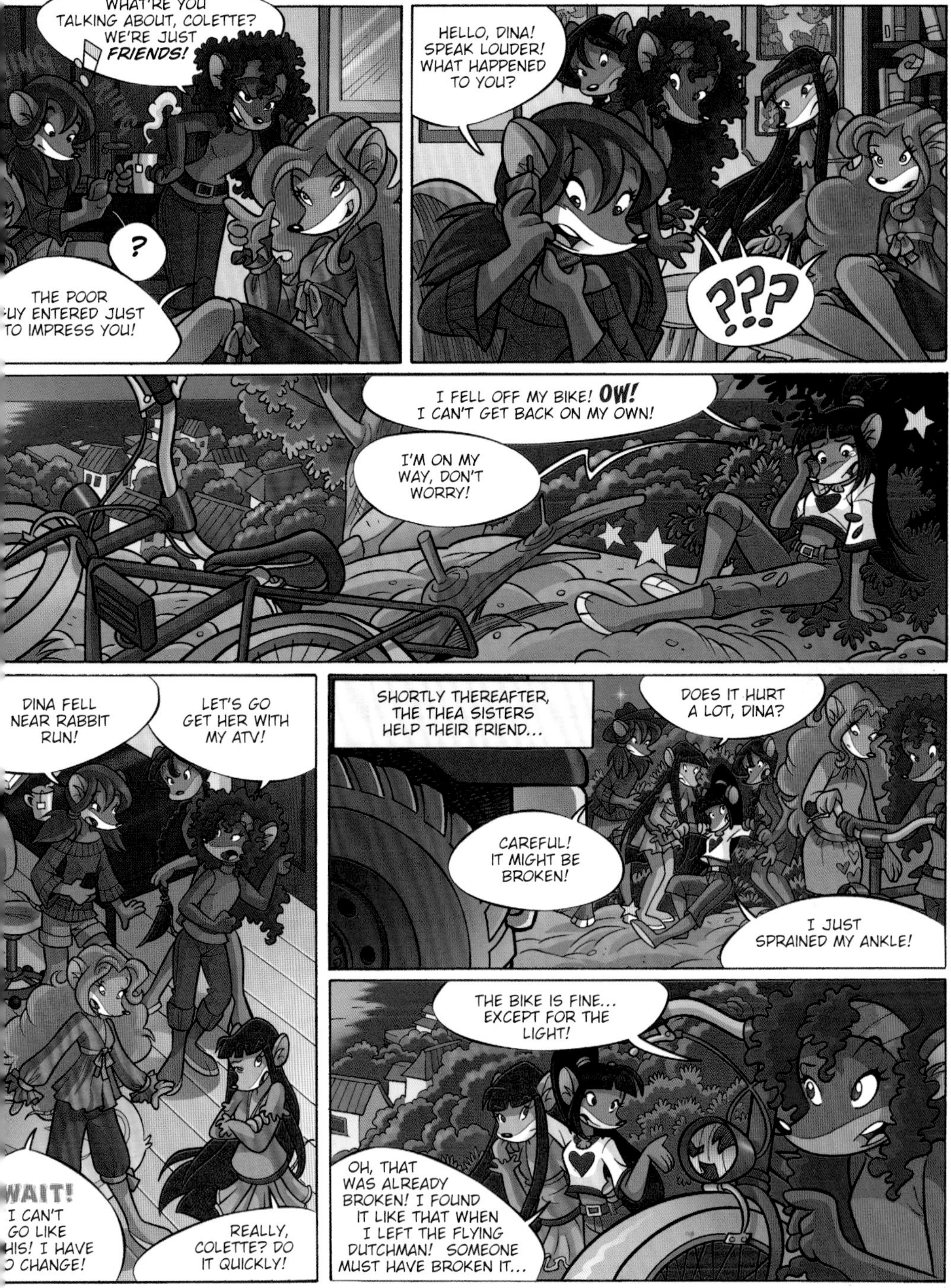
WHAT'RE YOU TALKING ABOUT, COLETTE? WE'RE JUST FRIENDS!
?
THE POOR GUY ENTERED JUST TO IMPRESS YOU!
HELLO, DINA! SPEAK LOUDER! WHAT HAPPENED TO YOU?
???
I FELL OFF MY BIKE! OW! I CAN'T GET BACK ON MY OWN!
I'M ON MY WAY, DON'T WORRY!
DINA FELL NEAR RABBIT RUN!
LET'S GO GET HER WITH MY ATV!
WAIT! I CAN'T GO LIKE HIS! I HAVE O CHANGE!
REALLY, COLETTE? DO IT QUICKLY!
SHORTLY THEREAFTER, THE THEA SISTERS HELP THEIR FRIEND...
DOES IT HURT A LOT, DINA?
CAREFUL! IT MIGHT BE BROKEN!
I JUST SPRAINED MY ANKLE!
THE BIKE IS FINE... EXCEPT FOR THE LIGHT!
OH, THAT WAS ALREADY BROKEN! I FOUND IT LIKE THAT WHEN I LEFT THE FLYING DUTCHMAN! SOMEONE MUST HAVE BROKEN IT...

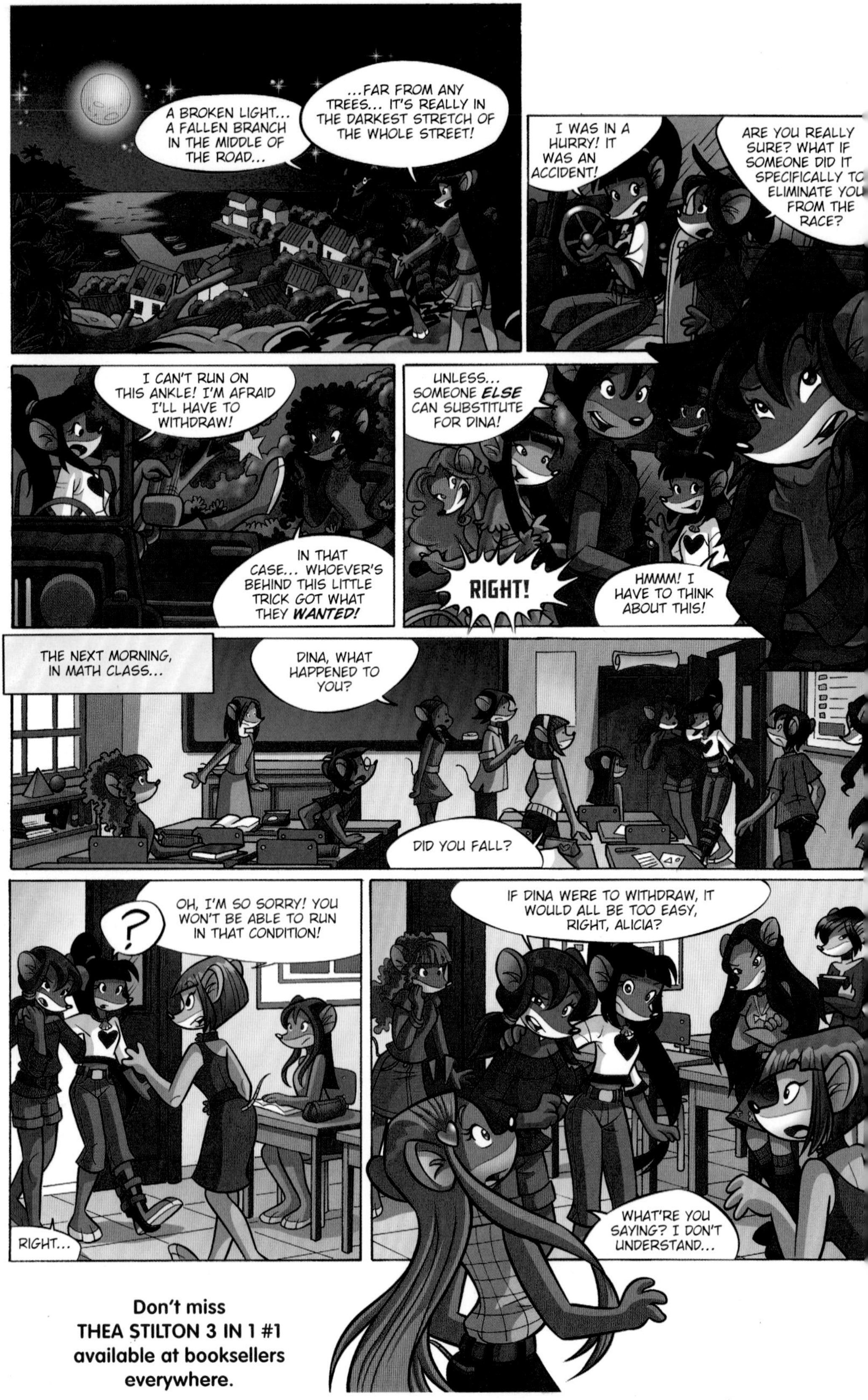
A BROKEN LIGHT... A FALLEN BRANCH IN THE MIDDLE OF THE ROAD...
...FAR FROM ANY TREES... IT'S REALLY IN THE DARKEST STRETCH OF THE WHOLE STREET!
I WAS IN A HURRY! IT WAS AN ACCIDENT!
ARE YOU REALLY SURE? WHAT IF SOMEONE DID IT SPECIFICALLY TO ELIMINATE YOU FROM THE RACE?
I CAN'T RUN ON THIS ANKLE! I'M AFRAID I'LL HAVE TO WITHDRAW!
IN THAT CASE... WHOEVER'S BEHIND THIS LITTLE TRICK GOT WHAT THEY WANTED!
UNLESS... SOMEONE ELSE CAN SUBSTITUTE FOR DINA!
RIGHT!
HMMM! I HAVE TO THINK ABOUT THIS!
THE NEXT MORNING, IN MATH CLASS...
DINA, WHAT HAPPENED TO YOU?
DID YOU FALL?
?
OH, I'M SO SORRY! YOU WON'T BE ABLE TO RUN IN THAT CONDITION!
RIGHT...
IF DINA WERE TO WITHDRAW, IT WOULD ALL BE TOO EASY, RIGHT, ALICIA?
WHAT'RE YOU SAYING? I DON'T UNDERSTAND...